Christmas Lights

BY
CHARLES HECHT

ISBN-10: 1481061100
EAN-13: 9781481061100
Library of Congress Control Number: 2012922233
CreateSpace Independent Publishing Platform
North Charleston, South Carolina

To Ellen

Nat Alone

NAT ZEIGLER SAT ALONE IN his house. He took off his reading glasses and placed them beside the lamp. About to rub the bridge of his nose with his thumb and index fingers, he stopped. Forty-five years as a printer had made him ever wary of his once ink stained fingers and he let the newspaper drop onto his lap. It seemed to him that the news hadn't changed a bit in all of his seventy-five years. War, famine, deceit, and death. The names changed. The places too. But the stories had seemed to be the same for as long as he could remember.

People talked about the world having changed over the course of his lifetime. He wasn't so sure about that, at least not where it counted most to him. The way he figured it, there were good people and bad, and always would be. What hadn't remained the same was his world, the one whose borders enveloped his very own day to day existence. Oh, how that had changed with her absence.

Nat Zeigler had never thought that Ida, his wife of so many years, would die before him. She had taken such good care of herself. It was he who had smoked and taken a drink now and then. In the four years since her death he had become a virtual recluse. His two sons called, but they lived far away and with busy lives and families of their own, they seldom had the opportunity to see him. In the beginning, his and Ida's friends had tried, to call, to invite him over, to entice him out of the house. He seldom returned their calls and he never accepted their invitations. They tried to help. But he didn't know how to help himself and eventually they stopped trying.

Only twice a day, every day for the last four years, did Nat venture out of the house. He rose early every morning, and walked two blocks to the stationery store for his newspaper. Then he sat for the rest of the day in his well worn armchair, reading the paper or listening to a favorite radio station. He dozed off from time to time. At dusk he ventured out a second time. This second walk led him three doors down from the stationery store to his evening meal.

He ate in the same restaurant every night of the week. A bowl of soup, some rolls with butter, and a half a roast chicken or egg omelet on alternate days. He had never planned meals, done the food shopping, or cooked when Ida was alive. The kitchen was her domain. When she died, he did not have the inclination to do any of that. He told himself that he was too old to start such things. He simply learned to purchase household necessities such as milk and bread and coffee. He kept things simple during the day and headed out each night for his evening meal.

Actually, eating out gave him an excuse to leave the house. It gave him something to look forward to towards the end of the day, a daily destination of sorts in his life. He had never eaten in that particular place before Ida died, either alone or with her. In fact, he and Ida had seldom eaten out, anywhere. He had entered that restaurant by chance one day on a sweltering summer's morning. He was in need of a glass of water before returning home with his newspaper and a waiter was kind enough to give him one. And now that restaurant had grown in familiarity to become a necessary link in the routine chain of events that marked his daily existence. He had grown accustomed to its lack of ambience. Its dimly lit interior matched well his state of mind. He sat at the same table in the same seat nightly. He'd gotten used to the scratched formica tabletop, the creased and faded vinyl upholstery on the chair. The walls were windowless, the linoleum floor had long ago turned from beige to brown. Old, used, worn, and progressively fading. Nat Zeigler had stumbled upon the perfect surroundings to complement the way he felt about himself.

But this was not the only allure that the place held for him. As he had grown accustomed to the restaurant, so had its owner and waiters grown accustomed to him. He was a 'regular' and was treated accordingly. A friendly salutation, and more, was to be expected.

"How are you this evening Mr. Zeigler?"

"What will it be tonight Mr. Zeigler?"

"Can I get you anything else Mr. Zeigler?"

"Have a good evening Mr. Zeigler. We'll see you tomorrow."

It made him feel good, at least for a moment, to hear these simple inquiries and friendly words. He spent his days alone, feeling bad about things he could not express. His loss that had driven him to silence. His children that he didn't see. The silence that had cost him the companionship of friends. So it was here amongst strangers that he received a nightly dose of acknowledgement. It was here that he heard his name spoken. Here that he received a greeting, was fussed over and bid goodnight.

He needn't say much of anything to anyone here. This suited him perfectly. A quick yes, a nod of the head, a short lived smile. Nothing emotionally strenuous was required of him. Certainly no serious inquiries need be answered regarding how he was feeling, or moreso, not feeling. For that would have been the more appropriate question.

"So Mr. Zeigler, how are you not feeling today?"

"Funny you should ask that. Or maybe not so funny. I'm not feelin' so energetic, or useful, or happy. I'm not feelin' like I have anything to look forward to. Ida's gone and I never did adjust to that. Been lonely. No interest any more in the things I liked to do. Like reading a good book. Or gardening. You know I used to grow the best tomatoes around. Grew 'em from scratch. Started with a buncha seeds and ended up with the best tomatoes in the neighborhood. Never had a bad season. Usually had so many tomatoes that I gave most of 'em to the neighbors. Ida's gone and so is the garden. Backyard is nothin' but weeds now. The old neighbors either died or moved to warmer places. Too cold for 'em here in winter. Young people movin' in more and more now. I'm seventy-five and alone. So what else can I say? What's the world need with an old man like me anyway? By the way, you've been my waiter for almost four years and I like you, but that's quite a personal question to ask a customer. 'So Mr. Zeigler, how are you not feeling today?'"

"Sorry Mr. Zeigler. Let me start again. Good to see you Mr. Zeigler. How are you this evening?"

With a wan smile, Nat could simply nod his head to this one.

A Fork In The Road

$\mathcal{A}$s SATURDAY EVENING APPROACHED, FOLLOWING a gray February afternoon, Nat peered out from his window. He looked out across the street at the bright Christmas lights adorning the brick tudor directly opposite. Though Christmas and New Year's Day had both come and gone, Nat knew that his neighbor, Gus, never took down his lights with any great urgency. For all that it mattered to Nat, Gus might as well have taken them down four years ago…for good. Four long years ago, his last Christmas celebration with Ida, the final one before holiday cheer turned into a hospital vigil. "Gus oughta get 'em down already. Save a heck've alot on his electric bill," mumbled Nat. The words sounded familiar to him. "Say the same thing every year. Nobody listens. None a my business, I guess."

Nat shrugged his shoulders and reached down, clicking off the radio. It had just broadcast the approach of a snowstorm, yet the expectation of heavy snow did not deter him from his evening's destination. Standing at the window, he spied a few errant flakes swirling around in the wind. He donned his overcoat, hat, and scarf. Upon reaching for the door, he heard the ring of the telephone. Might be one of the boys, he thought to himself. He shuffled to the kitchen, removed his hat, and grabbed the receiver.

"Nat Zeigler here," he muttered into the phone.

"Hey pop, it's Bobby."

"Robert, my boy." Nat's voice rose ever so slightly. "Thought it might be you or Michael. How's the wife and the little ones?"

"They're not so little anymore, pop."

"Guess not," whispered Nat. "Time goes. It just goes."

"Listen, pop. We heard the weather report for New York. A major storm is heading your way. I spoke with Michael today and we're all worried about you. We know you like to go out for a walk every day, but considering the weather, maybe you should scale back a little bit."

"Ah, my boys," Nat sighed, speaking to himself as well as Bobby, "always worried about the old man. You're good sons. Your mom was always proud of you. May she rest in peace."

"So you'll stay in, pop?"

"See what I can do, Bobby. You'll kiss the little ones for me?"

"They're not so little," Bobby laughed. He paused a moment, hesitated and then continued, saying again what he had often said before.

"You know, pop, you wouldn't have to deal with that New York weather if you'd just move out here and live with us. You know we have plenty of room and would love to have you."

"Always invitin' me. Michael too. Both of you and your lovely wives. Can't do it Bobby. You and Michael are where you oughta be. Good jobs. Raisin' your family in a nice place. Your mother always said you boys were wise to take those jobs.

Funny how both of you got them offers one right after the other. She said, 'Nat, we have to let 'em go.' She cried but she was a wise one, your mother. And me, maybe not so wise. But this is where I belong, where I oughta be. In my house, the only place I know."

"I know pop. Just take good care of yourself and be careful. We all love you."

They said goodbye to one another. With a deep sigh, Nat put his hat back on. He adjusted it along with his coat and scarf, and headed once again to the door.

"Boys mean well," he mumbled, turning the door knob. "Always lookin' out for the old man. Don't want to be a burden to my kids though. Better I'm here. I'll be alright. Got my sea legs. Know my way around. Snow or not."

With the wind at his back, Nat scurried to the restaurant. From his window, he had seen but a few flakes of snow. He barely noticed that those few flakes had quickly become a flurry in the span of a few blocks.

He ate as deliberately as always, oblivious to the escalating snowfall outside. Certainly he had listened to the weather forecast. Surely, all of his life he had listened to the daily weather forecast. Once these forecasts had meant something to him. Perhaps determining what he might do or not do that particular day, or helping to decide what to wear or not wear. Whether to bring an umbrella or not; to take a light jacket or a heavier coat. None of that mattered anymore. No appointments, no job, no responsibilities. It could rain, snow, or do nothing of the sort. It did not matter to Nat. In winter he wore a coat, in summer he did not. No matter what the person on the radio said, for him the forecast would always be the same, day after day. Nothing but more loneliness and solitude, arriving from all directions and remaining...indefinitely.

❄❄

He finished dinner and reached for his overcoat, barely glancing outside.

"Goodnight, Mr. Zeigler. Get home safe."

The waiter's words trailed behind him as he pushed open the door. He walked into a white wall of snow with little visibility ahead. He raised his coat collar, puffed his scarf up under his chin, and lowered his hat over his eyes. Against a determined wind, every step forward consumed the energy of two. Each glance up and ahead proved of no use. The gusting wind irritated the rims of his eyes as he tried to pierce the veil of snow. His breathing becoming labored, he plodded on. Unable to see clearly ahead, enveloped in a whirlwind of white, he tried to navigate the streets which he thought led home. He made a mistake, crossing the street at a familiar fork and veering to the left instead of the right. He had traversed that intersection countless times in the past. But never before had he been so breathless, tired, and disoriented.

Suddenly, he imagined seeing dimly lit colored lights flashing through the white shroud. Gus's Christmas lights? Must be, he thought. "Just gotta head straight to 'em and cross over. Be home in no time," he puffed into the frigid air. He continued on. Made weary by bracing against a relentless wind, Nat only wished for shelter. With his vision now cast downward in defense of his eyes, he walked into a circle of light formed by an overhead streetlight. He leaned against the lamppost, wrapping his arm around it and gripping the cold steel. A few moments later, with a deep sigh, he readied himself to move on.

The intent to proceed was arrested by the sudden sensation of someone or something gripping his left elbow. He felt the burden of supporting himself partially alleviated.

"Come inside with me," whispered someone.

Nat was aware of a man trying to look directly into his face.

"Come inside with me," said the man, "my name is Stephen Brook. I live right here. That's my wife Lila."

Nat looked to where a woman was standing in a doorway, her arms folded across her chest, shivering.

"Please hurry!" she called, her plaintive cry no match against the howling wind.

Nat saw Stephen glance in her direction.

"I'll be o.k.," he faintly breathed, his voice muffled by his scarf. He looked up squarely at Stephen, his eyes red and irritated, his cheeks tear stained. Flashing through his mind were all of those sensational newspaper stories he had ever read about chance encounters leading to no good end.

Stephen gently tugged on Nat's elbow.

"Please come inside with me," he implored.

"I'm almost home," murmured Nat. "I'm sure of it."

"Just for a while then," continued Stephen. "Just to warm up."

Completely depleted, Nat relinquished his grip on the lamppost and let Stephen lead him up the walkway. As they approached the front steps, he saw Lila reaching out towards him. He let her take his right arm as he ascended the steps. Supported by Stephen and Lila, Nat entered the house and collapsed onto the living room couch.

"Oh my, you poor man," whispered Lila. "I'll put up some hot water for tea. Let's get something in you to warm you up."

Nat recognized that voice from outside in the snow. He glanced up at her. "Thank you," he said, slowly loosening his scarf.

"Take off your hat and coat," said Stephen.

"No, I can't stay.... Maybe a few minutes is all."

Nat was beginning to catch his breath. His tone becoming steadier, more measured.

"Can't impose, no," he continued. "I was almost home. Thought I saw my neighbor's Christmas lights. Don't have much stamina left. Must be seein' things besides."

"No, you saw Christmas lights alright," said Stephen. "Our neighbor Lenny puts up such a display that by the time he gets it all taken apart and down, it's just about time to put back up." He paused for a second. "No, you're not seeing things," he offered.

Nat barely heard Stephen speaking. He had closed his eyes and sank back into the soft cushions of the couch. He rested. Within minutes, the teapot whistled. Startled, he abruptly opened his eyes and turned in the direction of the high pitched sound, expecting Ida to appear any second. A moment later Lila exited the kitchen and approached him.

"Careful, don't burn yourself," she said, handing him the cup and saucer.

He took it from her. The cup rattled upon the saucer as his hand trembled.

"Thank you. It's kind of you."

"I didn't know if you took sugar or not. I could get some if you like."

"No, plain is just fine," he answered.

He sipped his tea and slipped into his own thoughts, staring into his teacup as Lila and Stephen watched in silence. Old and useless he thought to himself. So old I couldn't even get myself home in the snow. Coulda died on the sidewalk. Been in tomorrow's newspaper. Front page maybe. I can see the headline now. OLD MAN FOUND DEAD IN SNOW. Simple walk home and I couldn't do it. Good for nothin' is what I am.

"How about another cup?" Stephen broke Nat's train of thought.

"The pot is still on," said Lila soothingly, a gentle smile concealing her chagrin at the sight of the dazed, elderly man slumped on her couch.

"You're both too kind. Nothin' like that ever happened to me before. Been out walkin' day after day in all kinds of weather. Never bothered me before. Gotten old and just have to face it. Another cup of tea. Yes, that would be nice. You make a good cup of tea."

He looked at Lila.

"My wife Ida makes a good cup of tea, too."

He caught himself and hesitated for a moment.

"Made a good cup of tea I mean. Knew just the way. Knew just how long to soak the teabag."

Tears welled up in his eyes.

"I better go," he said suddenly.

He started to rise. Lila walked across the floor and sat beside him, gently placing a reassuring hand on his forearm as he slouched back onto the couch.

"What is your name?" she asked, her hand still resting lightly on his arm.

He leaned forward.

"Here, let me take that." Lila took the teacup from his hand.

"Thank you," he answered. "Nat, Nat Zeigler. I live right across the street. Surprised I've never seen you folks before." He looked from one to the other.

Stephen extended his hand to Nat.

"I'm Stephen Brook and this is Lila. But we've never seen you before either. You did say that you go walking every day."

"Right up this block," answered Nat. "Right up Birch Road every single day."

Stephen looked at Lila. Her eyes met his.

"Nat," she said softly, "this is Sycamore. Maybe the snowstorm threw you off a little bit. My guess would be that you were walking and when you came to the fork you went left instead of right. I don't think that would be hard to do in a snowstorm like this and it would bring you down our street."

Nat looked down into his lap in despair.

"Sycamore," he muttered to himself. "Sycamore and not Birch. How could I make a mistake like that? How?"

Stephen got up and walked over to the window. He stared out at the falling snow.

"There's no visibility at all," he said. "None at all. I can't remember the last time we had a blizzard like this."

Lila looked at Nat, who, with a glance in Stephen's direction, just continued to mumble.

"Sycamore. I can't believe I was on Sycamore! Seventy-five years old and I got lost. Lost in my own neighborhood. Livin' here for years and can't find my way home! I mean you get old you can't find your eyeglasses. Put 'em down and walk away. Five minutes, no one minute later you can't remember where you put 'em. Maybe boil a pot of water on the stove. Go do something else meantime and forget the water. Those are normal things. At seventy-five these things are bound to happen. But get lost in your own neighborhood. Can't find your house. It's not like lookin' for a needle in a haystack." He stopped and smiled half-heartedly. "You're very patient to sit here and listen to a foolish old man carrying on."

"You're anything but," Lila quickly admonished him, smiling and shaking her head, pointing her index finger in his direction for emphasis. "That fork could fool anyone," she continued reassuringly. "I can't tell you how many times Stephen and I have driven home late at night and gone left instead of right. I mean everybody takes the wrong fork at least once in their life. Wouldn't you agree?"

With a mixture of appreciation and understanding, Nat's half-hearted smile metamorphosed into a sincere grin.

"Maybe even more than once," he responded.

"Now, how about that second cup of tea?" asked Lila. "I'd be happy to get it for you."

A Sleepless Night

"WE CAN'T SEND HIM BACK out in the snow," said Lila, nodding resolutely.

Stephen and Lila stood together in the kitchen. Nat was in the living room sipping his tea. Stephen glanced out of the kitchen window.

"Nobody should be out in this," he began, "but...he is a stranger and..."

Lila didn't give him a chance to complete his sentence.

"I'll make up the extra bed, Stephen. Why don't you talk to him? He has to stay."

As she had expected, Nat's pride would not hear of it. But it was clear that his body was all ears. He simply could not move. A combination of physical exhaustion, hot tea and a warm cozy room, made him as immobile as a piece of heavy furniture. Stephen had only to ask once.

"Alright, I'll stay, I guess. I really shouldn't. I've imposed enough." Nat scratched his head.

"What'll I sleep in?" he asked, beginning to grin.

"What do you usually sleep in?" asked Stephen.

"Well, I don't usually..."

Lila walked in from the spare bedroom. Nat had stopped in mid-sentence, blushing. Stephen smiled to himself as Lila spoke.

"The bed is all made up. You are staying, Nat. Aren't you?"

"Sure am," answered Nat, his voice rising, akin to the rising level of comfort that he felt there.

"Stephen can lend you a pair of pajamas." She looked from one to the other. They nodded in agreement.

❦❦

Stephen gave him a bathrobe as well as pajamas. Lila left him a fresh towel on the bed and a glass of water on the night table. He said good-night, thanked them once again, and closed the door of the bedroom, exhausted. He undressed and draped his clothing over the back of an armchair sitting in a corner of the room. He put on the pajamas and sat on the edge of the bed. A small lamp on the night table dimly illuminated the room. He did not take note of his surroundings or whether the pajamas were a good fit. He was too tired to check out either. He took a sip of the water, clicked off the lamp and stretched out in the bed, pulling the blanket up to his chin.

He closed his eyes and let his thoughts roam to a familiar place. In his mind's eye he saw the darkened rooms of the house that he could not reach. He pictured his reading glasses and newspaper exactly where he had left them. Why shouldn't they be! The wedding picture of Ida and him sat on the bedroom dresser where it had always been. From room to darkened room his mind roamed, checking that everything was as he had left it. And then suddenly, lying in that strange bed, he was struck with an overwhelming sense of anxiety and fear. He began to perspire profusely. He could not remember the last time he had spent a night away from home. Certainly not once in the last four years since Ida's death. What if, he wondered, he never got home again! What if, he worried, he should die, right here in a strange room during the night! What would become of his possessions? The pictures, the letters, the million and one personal things that were his and Ida's. Ah, but the boys would come and collect them. But, but…had he locked the door behind him? What if he hadn't? Would everything be safe? What if someone broke in and took all that he cherished? What if… his thoughts spun on and on, entwining him in a web of fear. He wiped the sweat from his brow with the palm of his hand. He pushed off the blanket. Fitfully, he opened his eyes and just as quickly closed them again. He tossed about, and finally, after turning from side to side and back again, he dozed off. He slept, neither deeply nor with any tranquility.

Lila too had difficulty falling asleep. She lay awake thumbing through a magazine while Stephen slept beside her. She flipped through the pages, unable to focus on any of the articles and just barely glancing at the pictures and advertisements. She finally put the magazine aside. Her instincts impelled her to check on Nat. The same instincts, perhaps, that drew her to the living room window where she first spied Nat out in the storm. She quietly got out of bed, careful not to disturb Stephen. She put on her robe and tiptoed out of the room. After switching on the hallway light, she reached for the door to Nat's room. His labored breathing accosted her ears even before turning the knob.

As she gently pushed open the door, the light from the hallway slowly swept across the room. As the light fell across him, she could see that Nat was drenched in sweat. His hair was wet and pasted to his brow, the pillow soaked through where his head lay. Alarmed, she walked to his bedside and felt his forehead. He was burning with fever. She was sure of it. He opened his eyes to her touch. He stared past her, vacantly, and then closed them. She left the room.

"Stephen, wake up!"

Lila grabbed his shoulder and shook him. He opened his eyes and bolted upright.

"What is it? Is everything o.k.? What time is it?"

"It's Nat. He looks awful. He must be running a fever."

"Is he awake?"

"No. He's sweating terribly."

"Why don't I put up some hot water for tea. It seemed to do him good before."

"Put a little brandy in it," said Lila. "It might help. I'm going to take his temperature and try some cold compresses."

Stephen got up, threw on his clothes and headed to the kitchen. As he passed Nat's room, he peeked in for a moment.

"You'll be o.k.," he whispered. "Lila will take good care of you."

Lila got a thermometer and returned to Nat's room. Briskly, she shook out the thermometer. Meanwhile, Nat had opened his eyes and with a great effort, propped himself up on his elbows, coughing.

"Winter is gonna kill me yet. I shoulda gone south with the rest of 'em," he grumbled.

"Here, Nat. Open your mouth."

Lila placed the thermometer in his mouth and a wet, folded washcloth, which she had also brought, across his forehead. He continued to grumble.

"Shoulda left town. Big mistake."

The thermometer trembled between his lips.

"Don't talk, Nat." said Lila. "The thermometer is moving around and it's going to fall out of your mouth."

It did. Nat looked at her sheepishly. She just smiled.

"Never was a good patient. Gave Ida fits whenever I got sick. I was a stubborn one. Wouldn't ever listen. Wouldn't go to the doctor. 'Just make me some of your soup Ida and I'll be fine.' That's what I'd say. 'Just a bowl of your soup Ida and I'll be fine. Better than a doctor.' Yep, that's what I'd say."

"She must have been quite a woman, Nat."

"The best. Took care of me when I was sick. Worked all her life and raised two kids on top of that. Both turned out good. She never complained about a thing. Never. She was an angel." His eyes watered. Lila put the thermometer back in his mouth.

"Here," she said gently, "now no talking this time."

He complied. As he lay there, Stephen walked in with the tea. Nat grinned and pursed his lips as if to speak. Lila shook her finger at him for the second time that evening.

"Not a word now," she said, with a furrowed brow and a look feigning displeasure.

Stephen put the teacup on the night table.

"How is he?" he asked.

"We'll know in a few more seconds," answered Lila. She reached for the thermometer.

"One-hundred and two," she said calmly, hiding her alarm.

Stephen too tried to appear calm.

"I'll take the washcloth and make it colder. In the meantime Nat, drink some of that tea I brought you."

Nat took a sip and smacked his lips together.

"Some tea you make," he said, wide-eyed. "Special blend?"

Stephen smiled.

"Lila's idea," he answered.

"You're a lucky fella, Stephen. Your wife's a gem."

Lila's face reddened in embarrassment.

"I hope you never lose her," he continued.

"Never," responded Stephen. "Now you stop talking. I'll be right back with a fresh compress." He turned and left.

Nat did not take his advice.

"You know, you remind me of my Ida," he said, looking at Lila. "She was a gem, too. But there I go mentioning Ida again. I don't know how many times it's been tonight! Haven't really talked to anyone in years. Let alone about... Not since the day she..." After faltering, he coughed several times.

"Please, you must rest," Lila importuned softly.

Stephen returned with a fresh, cold washcloth, and placed it across Nat's forehead. Nat looked at him and then closed his eyes. Stephen walked to the other side of the bed and stood beside Lila.

"Poor man," he whispered, "he's had a hell of a night. Wandering around in a blizzard. Now a hundred and two temperature. I'm glad we could help him out. I'm sorry I even hesitated..."

Nat was now sleeping, his breathing no longer fitful, but becoming more steady and rhythmic. Lila turned to Stephen.

"Maybe he'll sleep through the night. Or at least what's left of it."

"I could use a little sleep myself," said Stephen. He peered out of the bedroom window. The snow was falling with the same intensity as when he had first encountered Nat. "Thank god it's Saturday," he continued. "Or I guess Sunday now. It would be tough even trying to get to work today."

"Why don't you go back to bed. I'm going to stay up and keep an eye on him. There's no use in both of us staying up."

"Do you think he'll be alright?" asked Stephen.

"I hope so," answered Lila.

They quietly left the room. Lila returned moments later. She pulled the chair from the corner of the room to the side of Nat's bed and settled into it. While leaning forward, she repeatedly tapped her chin with her index finger, pensively studying his face.

"What brought you to our doorstep, Nat Zeigler?" she whispered in the dark. "I wonder. Fate? Chance? Could there be a reason? I wish I knew. I wish I knew so many things."

Lila sighed deeply and yawned. She closed her eyes and shook her head from side to side.

"Loneliness is a terrible thing," she continued. "I guess it doesn't matter what age you are. Nobody is immune to a broken heart."

She opened her eyes and reached out, gently touching the side of Nat's forehead with the back of her hand.

"You'll survive the night," she said, her words resolute, though her voice still a whisper. "We'll bring down your fever. I promise. And as for your heart, we'll just see."

A New Morning

NAT ZEIGLER OPENED HIS EYES. A new morning had arrived. He raised himself on both elbows and looked around the room. The previous night's events did not begin to come into focus until he spied the thermometer and teacup on the night table beside the bed. He sat completely upright, stretched out his arms, and yawned. He felt pretty darn good. No aches. Not a pain. Certainly not a fever. He began to recall everything that had happened since he left the restaurant the night before. I shouldn't feel this good, he thought to himself. Not after what happened to me last night. But he did.

He felt as good as if his own Ida had nursed him through another winter's cold. So many colds had she gotten him through. So many bowls of her chicken soup had he consumed. Oh, if only chicken soup could have cured her ills. If only it had been that simple. Yet there had been nothing that could halt the deadly growth that had engulfed her body. He had felt so impotent at the end, resigned to sitting beside her and holding her hand. Watching her drift toward him in pain and then recede beyond his grasp. Watching her drift back to him and away. Over and over again. Finally she drifted too far away, too far ever to return.

He got out of bed and stretched again. With his arms fully extended to either side, his hands lay hidden in the pajama sleeves. He looked down. His feet had disappeared in folds of piled high material. Again, he looked around the room. He saw his clothes draped over the back of a chair. He scratched his head and looked quizzically at the chair. "Funny thing. That chair was over in the corner when I went to bed last night. How'd it get next to the bed?" He tilted his head to the side, perplexed. "I musta been dreamin'. Or was it a dream? And was it last night? Coulda been the fever. A young lady was sittin' in a chair. Just like that one. Just sittin' in the dark and weeping. She looked so sad. Looked like the sweet lady who helped me last night. What could she have been cryin' about? Mind must be playin' tricks on me. Too much excitement for an old man! Oh, well."

He walked to the window and peered outside. He hadn't any idea of the time. He wasn't even sure of the day. He tried to recall what he had eaten for dinner the night before. That would place him within a time frame, leading him to the correct day of the week. Within his field of vision he noticed a squirrel, running along a tree branch. It skipped to another branch and then to a fence, scampering along the pickets. From the fence it jumped to the roof of a shed and then disappeared out of sight.

Nat thought for a moment. The week had started out with an omelet on Monday. He was sure of that. Half a roast chicken on Tuesday. Back to an omelet on Wednesday. Chicken Thursday. He knew yesterday wasn't Thursday. But he did have chicken last night. Ah. That was it. Today was Sunday!

The squirrel re-appeared from behind the shed. No, he couldn't be sure if it was the same one. He watched as it jumped to the fence and raced along the pickets to the tree. It pulled up short, stopping dead in its tracks, and then lunged for a branch. Could be Monday, Nat thought to himself. No, no. The last newspaper he read had that comin' up on Sunday box on the front page. Yep. Definitely Sunday today.

Just then another squirrel emerged from behind the shed. Nat expected it to follow its predecessor. Instead it made its way onto a telephone wire and traversed the entire backyard. He lost sight of it in a tangle of trees, vines, and tall bushes. As Nat looked back across the yard, he realized for the first time just how much snow had fallen. Not only did his eyes meet a continuous blanket of white, but he was astounded to see the snow ascending in drifts of what must have been several feet against the sides of the shed. Suddenly there was a light tap on the bedroom door. Nat turned from the window.

"Come in," he called.

Stephen opened the door and took a step into the room.

"Thought you might be up already," he said. "How are you feeling this morning?"

"In much better shape than last night. That's for sure. Thank you again for helpin' me out. And your lovely wife."

"Don't give it a second thought. Say, that's really some pair of pajamas I gave you. Could use some alterations."

Nat grinned and threw his arms out to either side.

"Got a point there!" he exclaimed. "Brother-in-law was a tailor. Woulda had me hemmed up in no time."

They laughed together.

"Well, I'll let you pull yourself together," continued Stephen. "You know where the bathroom is. Feel free to shower. When you're ready, head into the kitchen. We'll all have breakfast together."

"You've been too kind," responded Nat. "I really don't think I should impose on you any more. That shower sure sounds good but after that I think I should be gettin' home."

"Nat, I hate to say it, but in all honesty I don't see how you're going to get home this morning. It might not even be possible at all today."

Nat took another look out of the window.

"Know what you mean. I haven't seen this much snow in years. Can't walk in it and I guess the streets haven't been plowed through yet." He shook his head from side to side. "Shoulda gone south! Don't you think?"

Nat hadn't turned from the window. There was a pause.

"So, what do you think?" Nat continued.

"Well," Stephen hesitated, "it's never too late to change your mind. I mean you never know what tomorrow will bring."

Nat continued to stare out of the window.

"Tomorrow," he whispered, with a shrug of his shoulders. "Can't think about tomorrow if all a fella's thinkin' about is yesterday."

Nat suddenly turned to Stephen with a broad smile.

"So, what's that lovely wife of yours got in store for us for breakfast?" he asked, his voice having risen.

"I hope you like homemade muffins."

"Sure do," answered Nat.

"And waffles and coffee."

"Boy, I can smell that coffee." Nat drew a deep breath. "Perked I'll bet. Right on the stove. Just like..." He stopped in mid-sentence, walked over to the chair and reached for his clothes. "Guess I oughta be gettin' dressed," he said.

"Head into the kitchen when you're ready," replied Stephen, as he walked toward the door. He seemed to sense that Nat no longer wished to speak.

Chicken Soup

"I CAN'T SAY ENOUGH FOR WHAT you two've done for me." Nat wiped the corners of his mouth with a napkin. "I haven't had a home cooked meal since, well since…hardly eaten with anybody in years."

"Would you like another muffin?" asked Lila.

"Oh, no thank you. Had two already. Darn good muffins too. Can't beat this coffee either!"

Nat leaned back in his chair, patted his stomach and cleared his throat.

"You know, I wouldn't a blamed you two if you hadn't helped me out last night. Hate to say it, but it's a crazy world. Read terrible things in the papers all the time. Never can tell what's gonna happen. I wouldn't a blamed you if you went back in the house and shut the door tight. Glad you didn't though."

"So are we," responded Stephen.

"Sometimes you just have to take a leap of faith." Lila spoke as she stood beside Nat, reaching over his shoulder and letting a waffle slide off of her spatula and onto his plate.

"Another one. Oh, my goodness!" he exclaimed. "I can't. I just can't. This has been a feast. I'm just not used to eating like this. And everything was so good. You oughta open up a restaurant."

Lila laughed.

"I love to cook, Nat. But not enough to give up teaching."

"Teachin'! Not surprised. Bet you take darn good care of the school kids!"

"She's a great teacher," said Stephen, his voice filled with pride. "She loves children."

"I'll bet she is!" exclaimed Nat. "She's a gem, your Lila."

Lila blushed. Nat continued.

"How about you, Stephen? What do you do for a livin'? Teacher too?"

"No, I'm a banker, Nat. Work for a large bank."

"Not a teacher too? You and Lila seem like two peas in a pod to me."

"I guess I could have been one. I've thought about it sometimes. Math perhaps. I like numbers, Nat. They're straightforward, uncomplicated. Black and white so to speak. No shades of gray. With numbers there's always an answer and I can always figure it out. I like things like that."

"Geez, a teacher and a banker! Two peas in different pods, I guess."

"I'm so glad that you're feeling better," said Lila. "If your fever hadn't come down, I'm not sure what we would have done. We were pretty much snowed in last night. We probably couldn't get out and no one was getting here."

"Chicken soup," smiled Nat.

"What was that you said?" Stephen leaned closer.

"Ida's chicken soup," sighed Nat. "Always worked like a charm. That woulda done the trick. It was the best."

Nat looked down into his cup, his smile turning to a frown as he stared into the black coffee.

Lila didn't hesitate.

"What we could do," she quickly suggested, "is make it for you. The three of us. If you know the recipe."

Lila suddenly glanced at Stephen, her eyes widening under raised eyebrows.

"Absolutely, Nat. Just say the word," he said, immediately recognizing the look that Lila had shot his way. He'd seen it often enough, her silent way of saying, "just trust me, trust me and come along."

Nat looked across the table directly into Lila's eyes.

"Know the recipe!" His face was aglow. "It's the only recipe of Ida's that I do know. Know it in my sleep. Boy, what I wouldn't give for a bowl of Ida's..."

He suddenly stopped, yielding to a sense of apprehension. Not since Ida died had he tasted her soup. Four long years. Not once had he thought to make it himself. He could still taste it, though. He could still close his eyes and inhale the steam that rose from the open pot. Why, why hadn't he reached into the back of the kitchen cabinet and pulled out that old soup pot? It had passed to Ida after her own mother's death, as had the recipe. He could still picture Ida hovering over that pot, tasting, sipping, turning to him with a ladle full of soup. He too would sip.

"So," she would say, "I'll run it through the strainer now and we'll eat."

"Perfect," he would answer, "just perfect."

What he wouldn't give for a bowl of that soup... But maybe, just maybe, thought Nat, you don't fool around with something that was perfect. Only Ida could make soup like that. Only Ida, standing in her kitchen. Over her pot.

Nat continued to look into Lila's eyes, even deeper. She looked back, reassuringly. Nat deliberated for a moment. She brought me into her home. She took good care of me. Made me a nice cup of tea. Took my temperature. Ida woulda liked her.

"Just a pinch of sugar!" he heard himself blurt out.

Stephen stared at Nat, puzzled.

"What did you say, Nat? I thought I heard something about sugar."

"Ida would always say 'just a pinch of sugar'. No salt needed in the soup mind you. But just a pinch of sugar. Got a big pot in one of those cabinets, Stephen?"

Stephen knelt down and opened the cabinet to the left of the sink. He reached in and turned to Nat with a large pot in his hand.

"What do you think, Nat?"

"It'll do fine," returned Nat. "Not a family heirloom by the looks of it, but it'll do the job."

Lila giggled. Nat turned to her.

"So, what d'you say?"

"Nat, I would love to. It would be an honor to make Ida's recipe."

"Now mind you, it's your kitchen. You're in charge. I'm what they call a con...consultant. That's it. Stephen'll be our food prep fella. How are you with a peeler?"

Stephen thrust out his arm and with his palm down, spread out his fingers.

"Steady as a rock," he answered.

"Oh my goodness!" shouted Nat. "The ingredients." He reeled off a list. "A chicken, an onion, two carrots, two celery stalks, pepper, sugar, fresh parsley, fresh dill."

He stopped, crestfallen.

"You wouldn't have all those things in the house, I guess."

"I've got every one of them," answered Lila, emphatically.

Stephen just stared at her, dumbfounded. A coincidence? Was she expecting him?

※※

"How is that, Nat? Did I forget anything?"

Lila had gathered all of the ingredients and spread them across the kitchen table. Nat took a gander across the tabletop.

"Looks good," he said, nodding his head up and down. "Let's get the skin off of that chicken and get it into a pot of water."

They all became quite busy. Lila skinning the chicken, Stephen peeling the carrots, and Nat consulting.

"First we bring the water to a quick boil and then skim any fat off the top."

"How do you want this onion?" asked Stephen. "Should I dice it up?"

"Nope, doesn't get diced or sliced or anything else," answered Nat. "Just take off the skin and we'll drop it in whole."

"How about the carrots and celery?"

"Those you can cut up. But not too small."

"Any suggestions for skimming the fat?" asked Lila.

"Just run a spoon across the surface. That'll do the trick."

"Carrots, celery, and onion are ready to go," chimed in Stephen.

"O.K.," responded Nat. "Put a hold on those for a minute 'til we see what's doin' in the pot."

He looked over Lila's shoulder and inhaled.

"Hmmm," he sighed, "just wait 'til we get everything else in there. Ready, Stephen?"

"I am if Lila is."

"I've gotten rid of all the fat I can," she returned.

"Then put in what you've got, Stephen, and lower the flame. It's got to simmer for about an hour and a half."

"Shall we add the spices now?" asked Lila.

"Pepper, parsley and dill go first," answered Nat. "That pinch of sugar goes last."

Lila began sprinkling a bit of each spice over the open pot while Nat looked on. He hovered over her as she flicked a pinch of this and a pinch of that across the water's surface.

"Ah, perfect, perfect," he whispered. "A touch more dill. Ah, ah, easy on the pepper. That's it. Now a drop more parsley and we're in business."

Stephen handed Nat the sugar bowl from the kitchen table. Nat reached in, and between his thumb and forefinger, took that pinch of sugar. Lila stepped aside and Nat put the finishing touch to Ida's chicken soup. He once again inhaled the rising steam. Stephen knelt down and reached into the cabinet, mumbling to himself.

"Where's the cover to that pot?"

He stood up, the cover in his hand, as Nat turned from the stovetop, blinking with tears in his eyes.

"Must be all that steam. Got me right in the face. What with that onion bobbin' around in there."

Lila handed him a napkin. He took it and dabbed at his eyes. Stephen covered the pot.

"Well, I'm exhausted!" exclaimed Nat. "Must be all catchin' up to me. Wouldn't mind lyin' down for a bit."

"Why don't you stretch out on the couch," suggested Lila.

"You two don't mind?"

"Go ahead," said Stephen. "Lila and I will clean up in here while you rest."

"Mind if I listen to a radio?"

"If we can find one," laughed Lila.

"How about the soup?" asked Stephen. "Anything else need to be done?"

"No, just let it simmer," answered Nat, weariness having crept into his voice. "Give a taste now and then."

"We'll keep an eye on it," said Lila. "Try to catch up to yourself. Maybe you'll even fall asleep and when you wake up you'll have a nice, hot bowl of Ida's chicken soup."

"That would be good," Nat yawned.

Lila turned to Stephen.

"Please give Nat a pillow and a blanket. Leave a glass of water next to the couch, too. It wouldn't hurt if he kept drinking. The more fluids the better."

Nat stifled a second yawn.

"You're too kind. How will I ever repay your kindness?"

Lila just smiled as Stephen led Nat into the living room.

"Just give me a few seconds Nat and I'll be back."

"Take your time buddy." Nat dropped to the couch.

He leaned back, thinking, as he yawned again and rubbed his eyes. Such kindness, he mused to himself. There wasn't a sound.

Can hear a pin drop, he thought to himself. So quiet. Quiet as my house. He scratched his head and wondered. Stephen and Lila must be about the same age as my boys, thirtysomethin'. No sign of kids around the house. Funny thing, Stephen did say Lila loved children. Hmm...

"I'm leaving you a glass of water," said Stephen, entering the room and drawing Nat away from his thoughts.

He placed the glass on the end table beside the couch.

"Don't forget what Lila said."

"Please thank her for me. Would you?"

"Absolutely."

"You're a lucky fella, Stephen. But I musta told you that already."

"I think you did, Nat."

"Well, it bears repeatin'."

"I think you're about done in, Nat. Let's get you settled."

Stephen helped him off with his shoes. Nat stretched out and pulled the blanket to his chin.

"I gotta close my eyes. I'm beat. Mind puttin' the radio on low. Doesn't matter what station. Just as long as someone is talkin'. Helps me to sleep. Thanks, buddy."

Stephen adjusted the radio he had dug out of a closet and closed the window blinds.

Nat was drifting off to sleep as Stephen left the room.

❀❀

Upon his return to the kitchen, Stephen walked up behind Lila as she stood over the stove, stirring the soup. He put his arms around her waist and kissed her gently on the side of her head, the familiar fragrance of her hair now mixed with just a scent of onion.

"I love you Lila Brook," he whispered in her ear. "You're a good soul."

She turned to him.

"I love you too, Stephen," she answered, tears welling up in her eyes.

"No crying, now." He gently wiped away her tears.

"I'm sorry, Stephen. Sometimes I just forget myself. I can't be strong all the time."

"You don't have to be."

"I've made things hard for you, lately. Haven't I, Stephen? Sometimes I feel so selfish."

"No, Lila. I wish you wouldn't say that. We all have our faults, but selfishness is not one of yours."

"You mean I have others," quipped Lila, the hint of a smile suddenly crossing her lips. "I'm only kidding, Stephen. Don't answer that," she quickly added.

"Well, let me see," returned Stephen. "You're smart and beau... Wait a second. You wanted faults. Didn't you?"

Tears returned to Lila's luminous blue eyes as Stephen continued.

"Seriously. We're always so busy. With our jobs and everything else that competes for our time. But you've always known what's important and that's what I've always loved the most about you. You don't even give a thought to how beautiful you are. You never have. I don't know, after all these years, if you even realize it. You never wear jewelry or make-up. You don't follow the latest style or fashion or trend. I mean I never know what to buy you for your birthday because none of those things have ever mattered to you. In a world that's all about image, Lila, you've truly got it right. You know who you are. I love your long hair and your blue eyes and your soft skin. But I love what's in your heart the most. Nat Zeigler is lucky to have met you."

Stephen enveloped her in his arms. She leaned her head against his chest.

"I'm so tired," she sobbed.

"I know you are," he answered.

Lila looked up into his eyes.

"Kiss me, Stephen," she said.

They kissed and held on to one another for a moment. As they embraced, the telephone rang.

"Let it ring," said Lila. "Let the machine go on. We'll call back later."

"Are you sure?" asked Stephen.

Just then they heard the distinct voice of Lila's mother.

"I'll get it," said Lila.

"Don't!" snapped Stephen, abruptly.

"Stephen!" shot back Lila, her blue eyes ablaze as she reached for the phone. With her other hand she brushed back her hair, composing herself.

Seldom did Stephen see that look, that fleeting flash of anger.

He sat down at the kitchen table, waiting uncomfortably and looking vacantly at the tabletop, listening to Lila's half of the conversation.

"I'm feeling alright, mom. No, nothing is new. He's fine. I will."

He looked up and remained silent, watching Lila as she stared straight ahead, wiping the same part of the countertop with a damp sponge, again and again as she continued to speak.

"You're feeling well? And dad? I'm sorry to hear that. Tell him that I hope he feels better. When will we see you? That long? Well, enjoy your trip. I love you too."

Upon hanging up the receiver, she turned to him and rubbed her forehead, sighing deeply.

"I know how you feel, Stephen," she said, "but she's still my mother."

Stephen shook his head.

"I know that, Lila," he responded, his words imbued with an unmistakable touch of sarcasm. "I'm sorry," he quickly apologized, "but they just make me so angry. With all that we're going through, they're never here. They're always somewhere else, doing something else. It's as if you're just an afterthought."

"They're retired, Stephen. They've worked hard and earned the right to enjoy themselves and travel and do whatever they want."

Lila paused, that momentary look of anger replaced by one of exasperation.

"I'm disappointed in them," she continued. "You know that, Stephen. But they're still my parents and I want to speak with them."

"It's not just that," answered Stephen. "They've always been so self-absorbed, especially your father. I don't understand why you defend them."

"I'm not defending them," countered Lila, emphatically. "I'm just trying to understand them. They're only human. I have to accept them the way they are. I've always had to do that."

"Well, considering our circumstances, why aren't they more supportive and understanding of you. A phone call now and then simply isn't enough."

Lila approached the kitchen table.

"Please, Stephen, stop. You're being unfair. I hate when we argue about this."

"I'm not unfair, Lila, but I'll stop. Not because I agree with you, but because I don't like to upset you. And...and...I should know better."

"Please, Stephen, don't do that to yourself."

"No, Lila, I should. How many years now has it been that my parents are gone. I still miss them. No matter what, you're lucky to have yours. I wish I could say the same. It's just...just that you deserve better from them."

"I miss them too, Stephen, but I don't feel the same about this as you do. Can we let it go for now? It doesn't make me feel better to talk about it."

"I'll try," Stephen relented.

"Thank you," Lila breathed with relief.

❀❀

Nat awakened to the familiar aroma of Ida's soup. He got his bearings and followed his nose to the kitchen. Alone in the kitchen, he peered at the simmering soup, then turned towards the door and listened. There wasn't a sound. He rummaged through the cabinets until he found a soup bowl. He got a spoon, then noticed a ladle Lila had left on the counter. He ladled himself out a sizeable portion of soup.

"Can't wait," he said to himself. "Can't even wait to strain out the vegetables."

He sat himself down at the table with the steaming bowl of soup. With his hand slightly trembling, he brought a spoonful to his mouth, blew on it and sipped. He closed his eyes. "Hmmm... The best Ida. Just the best there is."

Stephen and Lila had heard Nat. They couldn't help but peek in on him without his knowledge and didn't enter the kitchen until he had had that first spoonful of soup.

"Oh, sorry I didn't wait for..." he began, his face turning red in embarrassment.

"Don't even think about it, Nat," Stephen broke in, "you just eat. By the way, how is it?"

Nat just looked at Lila.

"I hope you don't mind that I went into your cabinets and all."

"Not even a thought," she answered. "How is the soup, Nat? Is it the way you remember?"

"Well, Nat. How is the soup?" repeated Stephen.

"Ida'd be proud," beamed Nat. "Now you two sit down and let me serve the both of you."

With barely a hesitation, he grabbed two bowls from the cabinet and two spoons. He filled each bowl with soup and put a piece of carrot in each.

"Enjoy!" he exclaimed, placing the bowls before them.

They sipped in unison. Nat waited for their appraisal. It was unanimous.

"Delicious," said Lila.

"No doubt about it," agreed Stephen.

Nat looked at them with a mixture of relief and skepticism.

"You're not just tryin' to humor an old man, are you?"

"Wouldn't think of it," answered Stephen.

"It's really good," said Lila. "Would you mind if I made it again someday? I don't think I'll ever forget the recipe."

"Don't mind at all. Anytime you like. The next step now is to refrigerate the rest of the soup. Pour it into containers and leave it in the refrigerator. The important thing to remember is that when you're ready to eat some more, skim the fat from the top before you pour it in a pot."

The three of them lingered in the kitchen, slowly eating their soup.

"Just before I dozed off I heard on the radio that another storm may be comin' on the heels of this one," Nat said, between sips.

"Maybe we should try and get you back to your own house before the next one hits," responded Stephen. "Not that we want you to leave, Nat," he quickly added. "You're welcome to stay as long as you like."

Lila nodded in agreement.

"Well, I'm feelin' much better thanks to the both of you. Probably should be headin' home soon."

"Take some of the soup home with you," suggested Lila. "You can have some tonight."

"Don't mind if I do."

Stephen rose from his chair.

"I'm going to have a look out the front window. See just how far we're going to get today."

He left the kitchen and subsequently called from the living room.

"The street is plowed. Might take me a little while to dig out the car, but I think we can get you home today."

Stephen glanced up at the sky. It was covered by an ominous blanket of clouds.

"Better get started on that," he said to himself.

Meanwhile, Lila and Nat had begun to clear the kitchen table.

"Do you have milk in the house and whatever else you might need?" asked Lila. "Just in case you get snowed in. If not, you're welcome to anything we have."

"I'll be o.k.. Thank you. I have milk, bread. I'll be fine."

Lila rinsed the bowls while Nat wiped down the table.

"Guess I should go pull myself together," he said.

"Go right ahead, Nat. I'll finish up in here."

Within the half hour Nat was sitting in the living room ready to go. Once again he was bundled up in his overcoat, hat, and scarf. Though this time, not tired, disoriented, or red-eyed.

"Ah, my soup!" he exclaimed, as Lila handed him a small package.

"You certainly look ready to go."

"I guess I do want to get home."

"Here. I want you to take this also."

She handed him a folded piece of paper.

"It's our phone number. If you ever need us, call. We're only a few blocks away."

Nat took the paper and tucked it in his overcoat pocket.

He looked thoughtfully at her for a moment.

"You know what? If you have another piece of paper handy and a pencil, I'll write mine down for you and Stephen. Just in case you two ever need me."

"That's a great idea, Nat," responded Lila, her voice rising as her eyes lit up.

Stephen walked through the front entrance as Nat was writing down his number for Lila.

"Car's all ready." He stamped his feet on the floor, shedding the snow from his boots.

"I guess I am too," said Nat.

He handed his phone number to Lila.

"Thank you…for everything." He extended his hand.

Lila shook it and then gently kissed him on the cheek.

He blushed.

❄❄

Stephen and Nat drove the few blocks to Nat's house. Stephen brought a shovel with them and while Nat waited in the car, he cleared a path to the front door.

"Thank you for all your help, Stephen."

They stood facing one another on the front porch.

"No problem, Nat. I just wish we had met under better circumstances. Are you sure you're feeling alright now?"

"I'm fine. Really. Don't worry about me. In fact, if you don't get goin' soon, I'm gonna start worryin' about you."

They looked out across the front yard. It had begun to snow again. They shook hands.

"Think I'll go in and put up some soup."

"Maybe I'll go home and do the same," said Stephen.

They parted, smiling.

A Tap On The Window

With a chink in his armor of solitude, Nat Zeigler settled into his armchair that wintery night. He leaned back and with the radio on low and the lamplight dim, dozed off. He awakened to the sound of tree branches, swayed by the wind, beating against the house. He awakened and instinctively reached for his reading glasses and his newspaper. Neither was at hand. He wondered what time it might be.

"Gotta be pretty late," he mumbled to himself.

Once again he reached out, groping for his glasses along the small table adjacent to his armchair. Instead of glasses, he grasped a folded piece of paper. He stared at it for an instant. It did not register. A note? A receipt? A phone number? When? Where? From whom? He unfolded it, paused and smiled. "Yes, I will call them soon." He closed his eyes and fell asleep, oblivious to the sound of the tree branches beating against the side of the house.

※※

He did not call them soon. He took the piece of paper and placed it on his bedroom dresser. He glanced at it daily, and daily he

45

was tempted to reach for it and pick up the phone. Yet, for Nat Zeigler, solitude was a greater lure than his brief respite from it. In fact, he did not consider calling without a modicum of guilt. To smile, to laugh, to crack a joke as in the old days? Had he the right to do so? She couldn't laugh. She couldn't smile. So why should he? To spend time in the company of others, to be cheered and warmed? No, it would not do. He had buried his cheerfulness with her, tossed away his laughter and told his last joke. It was his obligation to mourn. Forever, or so it seemed.

Melancholy defined him. It was just another garment that he pulled on over his head in the morning and wore for the day. It wasn't even black. Just colorless. Simply opaque. It blended perfectly with anything that he happened to be wearing. He took it off each night. Off came his pants, his shirt, his melancholy. He laid them each across the chair in the bedroom. He put them on again in the morning. Morning after morning. Day after day. And now year after year.

He genuinely wished to call them. If only he could. He had so enjoyed that morning. He had so enjoyed cooking Ida's soup. He had let himself remember and this time it felt good. This time it was not a remembrance bound wholly by serious contemplation. He had, in a small way, celebrated a part of Ida with others. He had finally let a memory escape his consciousness to find that it could bring joy. But it was only a lapse. An oversight. Disoriented from the previous night, he must have forgotten to dress properly that morning. Forgotten that one indispensable component to his wardrobe, his melancholy.

❀❀

Nat finished all of the chicken soup Lila had given him and by week's end felt as he had before the storm. His temperature had not returned. Once again he was ready to resume his daily ritual. The weather cooperated, the sun melting the snow. The sidewalks were cleared, making walking permissible once again.

With coat, hat, and scarf in place, he descended the front steps. A bright winter's day of crisp, cool air enveloped his face. He looked up at the sky and breathed in deeply. As he walked along, he thought of how content he felt to be doing so again. He grinned and wondered in amazement at how an old man could be so content in the familiarity of a routine such as his. In his youth familiarity and routine would have precipitated a rebellion on his part. In his youth, if someone had told him that one day he would be satisfied to simply walk to and from a stationery store, to and from a restaurant each day, he would have laughed. Redundancy was now a comfort to him. He was old. He sought nothing new.

❈❈

As Nat was descending his front steps, Lila was preparing her students for dismissal. Another week of school had come to an end and her third graders were now clamoring at their cubbies in a sea of coats, boots, gloves, hats, scarves, and backpacks. Lila was in the middle of the muddle, as usual.

"Now kids, everybody line up to go. Who's at the head of the line today?"

All hands went up. The children knew the routine.

Lila put her hands on her hips, cocked her head to the side, and pursed her lips in apparent disapproval.

The children giggled as Lila broke into a broad grin.

"It's my turn, Mrs. Brook!" shouted Molly, her purple gloved hand remaining aloft as all of the other hands dropped.

"Well then, everyone behind Molly. Skip to it!" clapped Lila.

Lila approached the classroom door, delivering a few last minute instructions as the children hurriedly got into line.

"Jenny, don't forget your glasses."

"Cory, remember to give that note to your mom. I need to know if she can chaperone next week."

"Michael, thank your mom for sending in the cupcakes and have a wonderful birthday party this weekend."

"I want to see all of your bright smiling faces here Monday morning."

"Yes, Mrs. Brook," they chimed in unison.

The bell rang and they marched out of the classroom.

Lila stood by the door and watched as the last child in line turned the corner and disappeared from her view. She sighed deeply, lingering for a moment as her thoughts turned to the weekend which loomed ahead, another weekend as empty perhaps as the hallway which stretched before her. She turned and walked back into the classroom, put a few errant books back on a shelf, and then straightened up her own desk. Reaching for her coat and scarf hanging on the wall hook behind her desk, she heard Maggie's familiar voice.

"Join us for a drink, Lila?"

Maggie stood in the doorway.

"Oh, no thank you," answered Lila without hesitation, as she turned around.

"Are you sure? We'd all love you to come."

"Thank you, Maggie. I appreciate it. But I...I'm just tired I guess. Maybe another time."

"You don't have to explain to me," Maggie interrupted. "I'll just tell the girls you can't come."

"You're an angel," responded Lila.

"Maybe next week," suggested Maggie.

Lila smiled as she buttoned the top button of her coat.

"Have a great weekend," she called, as Maggie turned to leave.

Lila grabbed her shoulder bag and walked across the classroom. Just before turning out the lights, she stopped in front of the crooked, tarnished mirror, hanging adjacent to the classroom door. She reached in her coat pocket and pulled out her wool hat. After brushing her long brown hair away from her face with her right hand, she put on her hat, tucked in any wayward strands of hair, and straightened it. As she stood in front of the mirror, she could not help but see in her reflection the dark circles that had, over time, appeared under her eyes. Yes, she was no doubt tired, but couldn't help wondering how many Fridays it had been since she had last gone out with her colleagues. She so wished to spend a carefree moment among friends, and though she enjoyed her younger colleagues, an afternoon at the bar no longer enticed her. She looked in the mirror and pursed her lips. She saw a young woman getting older, no longer finding fulfillment in the transient pleasures of youth. She wanted something else, a more permanent joy.

Turning from the mirror, she sighed and reached for the light switch. She clicked off the lights and left the classroom. Upon exiting the building, she descended the front steps, beginning her walk home.

Nat was just sitting down to dinner.

❧❧

"So, Mr. Zeigler, feeling alright I hope?" the waiter inquired.

"Better," answered Nat.

Ensconced in his regular chair, parked at that familiar formica topped table, Nat felt relieved.

"Were you sick, Mr. Zeigler?"

"A little. Ran a fever. But I'm o.k. now. Thanks for askin'."

"We were worried about you. Me and the rest of the fellas and ladies here. You left the other day just when the big storm started. Got worse and worse. We were worried you got caught in it. And then we didn't see you all this week. It's good to see you again, Mr. Zeigler."

Nat smiled. The waiter continued.

"You know, there aren't too many old timers around anymore. The older folks' kids have grown and moved away. Now the old timers are leaving. Going down south. Young people moving into the neighborhood all the time. Oh well, good to see you again Mr. Zeigler. What'll it be Mr. Zeigler? Half a roast chicken?"

Going south. Nat wondered. Maybe he should. Maybe he should just take the years left to him, pack them in that old trunk in the attic and ship them south. Sure, why not be alone in the sun year round. Alone here. Alone there. What difference would it make?

Shortly, his roast chicken arrived.

Not halfway through his chicken, he was distracted by a few sharp sounds. Sitting in close proximity to the front window, he glanced up from his plate toward it. There, tapping on the glass, stood Lila. Nat was startled to see a familiar face peering at him. He momentarily lost his composure, staring motionless as Lila waved to him from the window. Finally, he waved back to her and then, quite spontaneously, rose from his chair and beckoned her in.

One Good Invitation Deserves Another

"I HOPE YOU DON'T MIND," SHE said, approaching his table.

"No, no, not at all," he heard himself answer, rising and extending his hand to her.

Lila reached for it and at the same time gave Nat a kiss on the cheek. He blushed and then quickly pulled out a chair for her and waited as she put down her shoulder bag and took off her hat and coat. She draped her coat across the back of her chair and then sat down. Nat returned to his seat.

"Funny thing," she said, brushing the hair away from her face, "to run into you like this".

"How's that?"

"I don't usually come down this street. Once in a blue moon, really. I only come this way when I stay at school very, very late, and that doesn't happen often. This way saves me a few minutes going home, so I took it today. Just as I was passing by, I looked in the window and there you were. I really hope you don't mind, Nat."

It could not have felt stranger to him. Sharing his table with someone else. Being with another person in a place which had come to signify his solitary existence. And yet, though it felt strange, he did not feel bad.

"Would you like a piece of roast chicken?" he inquired. "Be glad to split it with you."

"That's sweet of you, Nat, but Stephen and I are going to eat dinner later."

Nat looked at his half eaten chicken for a moment, tore off a small sliver of meat, and looked across at Lila, his eyes twinkling.

"Better yet, give Stephen a call and we'll all eat together here! My treat!"

Lila must have looked surprised.

"No, really, I mean it!" exclaimed Nat.

He too was surprised, shocked by his own suggestion. Nonetheless, he kept going.

"Roast chicken all around. Nothing but the best for my friends. It would be my pleasure."

"You're sure, Nat?"

"Absolutely!"

"Great!" exclaimed Lila. She glanced at her watch. "I'll call Stephen. He should just be finishing up at the bank."

"You can probably use the phone up at the front counter. Just tell 'em you're with Mr. Zeigler. They'll let you use it." Nat grinned and quickly added, "Come to think of it, maybe you have one of them funny little phones in your bag. I see everybody talkin' on 'em."

Lila laughed.

"I do, Nat. If you'll excuse me, I'll go call by the door. I don't want to be rude."

Lila left the table. Nat just sat there, astounded at his actions. Amazed at the audaciousness of his invitation. Amused by the silliness of his grand gesture. Roast chicken all around, indeed, he thought to himself. A real sport you are, Nat old fella. Just tell 'em you're with Mr. Zeigler. You know, the Mr. Zeigler. Table number six in the corner. He could barely stifle a laugh. Maybe they would have brought a phone over to the table if he had asked. "Hold on a second, Lila. No need to use that funny little phone. I'll have 'em bring a phone over for you." Silly or not, he mused, his invitation still stood. He felt good about having extended it.

"All taken care of," said Lila, upon her return.

"I'm so glad," responded Nat. "You know what? I didn't even ask you if you wanted chicken. I mean you can eat anything you'd like on the menu. Still my treat."

"Chicken sounds just fine."

"Glad that's settled. So, how have you and Stephen been?"

"We've been…" Lila paused. "Alright, I guess," she finished, her voice barely a whisper.

Nat noticed the hesitancy in her voice and would have perhaps changed the subject if she hadn't done so.

"We tried calling you a few times during the week to see how you were feeling. Stephen was going to stop by your house tomorrow. We were getting worried."

"I'm sorry I worried you," responded Nat. "Don't hear the phone a lot, what with the radio on and dozing off all the time. You know I wanted to call you too and thank you again for all you did for me but I just…" He faltered.

"That's o.k., Nat," Lila said, filling in his pause. "Stephen and I know how appreciative you are. I'm just glad that you're feeling better. Stephen is going to be thrilled to see you again."

Nat grinned. He felt good. Better than good. Yet, he couldn't help wonder why these young people seemed to like him so much. Him, just an old lonely man with his life behind him and theirs all ahead.

"He shouldn't be long," continued Lila. "Why don't you finish eating. Your food is going to get cold."

"I'll have them warm it up. I'd rather wait for Stephen. That way we can all eat together."

"Do you come in here often, Nat? You seem awfully comfortable here."

"Every day. I have dinner here. In fact, the night we met I was coming back from here."

"You must like the food," laughed Lila.

"Enough to almost lose my life for it!" he exclaimed, laughing along with her.

They hadn't chatted for very long when Stephen appeared at the front entrance to the restaurant. Nat waved him over. He rose and extended his hand.

"Good to see you again, pal. Just sittin' and talkin' to your lovely wife."

"How are you?" asked Stephen, shaking Nat's hand.

"Been doin' o.k.."

Stephen pulled out the chair next to Lila's. He leaned towards her and kissed her as he sat down.

"How was your day?"

"Pretty good," responded Lila. "Emily finally knows how to write all of her letters in script. She was so proud of herself today." Lila beamed.

"That's wonderful," said Stephen. "You've worked so hard with her." He turned to Nat. "Emily is a little girl in Lila's class, Nat. She's been having a tough time with her writing."

"Not easy bein' a kid sometimes," said Nat. "Good for you Lila and good for Emily."

"Thanks, Nat. You're right, it isn't easy being a kid sometimes. It's not always easy being an adult, either," she added, her smile fading. She glanced at Stephen. He returned her glance. Nat noticed their silent exchange.

"So," said Nat, interrupting the momentary silence, "I promised your lovely wife dinner all around. On me. What'll it be, Stephen? Roast chicken is your best bet, but be my guest and order whatever you want."

"Whatever Lila is having will be fine with me."

"Chicken it is then."

Stephen and Lila ordered dinner. Nat sent his meal back to be warmed up. They waited.

"Funny thing," said Nat, finally letting his thoughts materialize into words. "Been eatin' here for so long. Strange sittin' across from two friends. Seems pretty good, though."

"Maybe we can do it again," replied Lila.

"Sounds good to me," agreed Stephen.

"A person can get used to doing things a certain way," added Lila. "The last thing we'd want to do is intrude on you or make you feel uncomfortable."

"I don't feel one bit uncomfortable. In fact, I've been wonderin' about somethin' and if it wouldn't make you uncomfortable, I'd like to ask you a question."

Stephen pursed his lips and glanced at Lila.

"Go ahead, Nat," she said, drawing an apprehensive breath.

"Well, considerin' all the attention you showered on me last weekend, I didn't pay as much mind to the two of you as

I should've. Maybe only thinkin' about myself. So, I've been wonderin', how'd you two meet anyway? A banker. A teacher. Figure you'd be travelin' in different circles."

Lila exhaled deeply. "Actually," she began, "I was fifteen and Stephen was seventeen when we met. It was during the summer. We worked together upstate at a children's camp. The kids came up from the city from some really poor neighborhoods. Most of them had hardly ever seen a lot of trees, let alone a lake and mountains. We were young and idealistic. Kids ourselves, I guess. We couldn't wait to see each other again after the summer."

"And here we are, twenty years later," Stephen broke in, smiling.

"I have a question for you, Nat," continued Lila.

"Fire away."

"How would you like to go ice skating with us tomorrow morning?"

"How would I like to what?" asked Nat, dumbfounded.

Stephen stared at Lila. Even he was surprised at her invitation. She just looked intently at Nat. Stephen picked up the ball.

"Ice skating, Nat," he said. "Lila and I planned on going tomorrow. Why not come along? It'll be fun."

"Me! Ice skate! Haven't done that in forty years. I can hardly stand up in my own shoes at my age. You want me to stand in ice skates and then move?" He chuckled. "They got two blades on the bottom, maybe?"

"Three for you," answered Stephen.

"What the hell!" Nat heard himself shout. "You got a deal." Excitedly, he thrust his hand in Lila's direction.

She quickly grabbed it and mustered all of her strength for a hearty handshake.

The roast chicken arrived.

Some Things You Don't Forget

"WHOAAA..."

"I've got you, Nat. Lila, quick, grab his other arm."

"I knew one blade wouldn't be enough!" screamed Nat. "Two maybe even wouldn't be enough. Three, just maybe three."

"We've got you," joined Lila.

"Slide your right foot out first," she continued. "Slowly. That's it. Now the left. Good. Good. You're doing fine. Sorry if I sound like such a teacher."

"Nobody let go," importuned Nat. "Stephen. Lila. Don't let go of the old man. The hip'll be the first thing to break."

"Nobody's going to break a hip, Nat," Stephen reassured him.

"What if we break through the ice?" asked Nat, his voice rising in fear. "We'll drown."

"But we're not on a lake." Lila rolled her eyes.

"Oh, yeah. Now don't make fun of the old man," frowned Nat. "Piece of cake," he continued, tentatively placing one foot in front of the other.

"Now don't get overconfident," cautioned Lila.

"But I'm still standin'. Haven't done this in forty years and I'm still standin'!"

"Being held up might be closer to the truth. Don't you think?" asked Stephen.

"Well, maybe so," responded Nat. "But you gotta give an old man credit. Now, why don't you two step away, give me some room and we'll see what gives."

Stephen and Lila looked at one another, apprehensively.

"Oh, come on you two," Nat pleaded.

"O.K.," said Lila, "but not for long."

"Only a second or two," said Stephen.

They released his elbows and slowly inched away. He spread his arms out to either side, trying to maintain his balance as if he was on a tightrope. He stepped forward. Right. Then left. Right again.

"Hey, hey, still on my feet," he chuckled. "Ready to glide now. Ready to glide."

"Lila," implored Stephen, shaking his head from side to side.

She stood, gazing at Nat, her eyes sparkling in admiration.

"Let him go," she calmly said.

Stephen clasped his hands together and looked towards the sky. Lila watched Nat, the hint of a smile beginning to cross her lips.

"That's it, Nat," she whispered.

He inched forward, steadily gaining confidence as he progressed.

"Must be like ridin' a bike. What d'ya think? I guess a fella don't forget some things."

"Don't talk while you're skating," called Lila. "Concentrate on what you're doing."

"Look straight ahead," added Stephen. "Don't look down at your feet."

"Same thing Ida used to say when we went dancin'," called back Nat, as he started to turn in their direction.

"No, no, don't look back. You'll lose your balance!" exclaimed Lila.

Stephen raced towards him as Nat tried to maintain his balance. As he wavered to the left, Stephen caught a hold of his right elbow and pulled him upright. Lila followed suit and grabbed Nat's other elbow.

"Whew, close call!" cried Nat.

"Ready for a rest?" asked Stephen.

"Might be a good time for it," answered Nat. "How about some hot chocolate? Lila?"

"Sounds wonderful."

"Hot chocolate then. All around on me. Could get used to treatin' you kids."

They entered an old, rustic pavilion which sheltered a food concession and a small wood burning stove. They slid three across on a wooden bench in front of a crackling fire.

"Cozy little place. Didn't take much notice of it when we came in to put the skates on," said Nat. "Too excited, I guess. Nice fire. Know what's even nicer?"

"What's that, Nat?" asked Stephen.

"The way you two've been treatin' me. Met a lot of people in my day, but I never took the measure of a person by how big their job was. Nope. It's how big your heart is. That's what counts. And you and the little lady, hearts of gold from where I sit. Bet your parents are prouda each of you."

"Thanks, Nat." Stephen's eyes quickly moistened as he stared at Nat. "My parents both passed away," he whispered.

Nat winced. "I'm sorry. Musta been hard. I'm sure you miss 'em."

"Every day."

"How 'bout Lila's folks? Hate to think the same."

Stephen's gaze dropped to his feet. He fidgeted uncomfortably on the bench.

Nat waited, perplexed, sensing that his question had somehow caused Stephen discomfort.

"They're fine...I guess," Stephen finally answered. "We don't see them too often, they're..."

"You two look serious," interrupted Lila, approaching the bench.

They both looked up toward Lila. She stood in front of them, in her outstretched hands she held a cardboard tray with three hot chocolates upon it.

"Thought I was treatin'," said Nat.

"When did you buy those?" asked Stephen.

"I snuck off when you two started talking. You didn't even notice. What were you two discussing, anyway? You both looked terribly serious."

"Not much," answered Stephen, not wishing to put a damper on the afternoon.

She placed the tray on the bench. Stephen handed her a cup, gave one to Nat, and then took the last for himself. He and Lila sipped theirs while Nat just held his cup and let the warm steam rise to his face.

Boy, pleasure bein' out with good people, he thought to himself. It's been so long. But I shouldn't stay away from the house much longer. I've got some cleanin' to do and I haven't read today's paper yet and I don't want to miss my four o'clock radio program and...I wonder what time it is anyway.

"Nat." Stephen lightly touched Nat's shoulder. "Nat, are you alright? You looked a little worried there for a minute."

"I, I'm o.k., Stephen. Just daydreamin' I guess."

"What do you say we get back on the ice," suggested Lila.
Nat hesitated.

"I don't know," he answered. "It's getting kinda late and it'll be dark soon."

"There's still a little more daylight," insisted Lila. "How about another one or two times around before we head home?"

"How about it, Nat?" Stephen also insisted.

"I see you two aren't gonna let me off the hook. Hey, why not! I just hope you two know a good orthopedist."

Under the waning light of a winter sky, they nearly glided across the ice. They skated three abreast with Lila in the middle. They held hands and practically skated in unison but for Nat's intermittent near falls.

"Just gotta smooth out the rough edges," he explained, as they rounded one end of the rink and retraced their path.

"And how long do you think that will take?" asked Stephen, good-naturedly.

Nat pondered for a moment.

"Probably more time than I've got." He laughed at himself.

"Well, that's two times around," said Lila.

"And you didn't fall once," marveled Stephen.

"Neither did you," shot back Lila, grinning. She reached across Nat and playfully pinched Stephen on his side.

"Hey, cut it out now!" cried Nat. "I don't want anybody lettin' go of my..."

Just then Stephen and Lila simultaneously let go of Nat's hands. A little girl had skated into their path and fallen just ahead of them. Nat stood frozen to the spot where they left him as they knelt beside the crying child. She lay face down on the ice. Stephen gently lifted her to her feet.

"Are you alright?" he asked softly.

She simply nodded in response, her cheeks wet with tears.

"Are you o.k., Kate?" someone asked.

Stephen and Lila turned toward the young woman standing beside them.

"Thank you so much," she continued. "Katie got a little bit ahead of me and before I could catch up..."

"You're very welcome," answered Lila, bending to brush the ice shavings from Katie's coat.

The little girl stopped crying and reached for her mother's hand. Stephen stood up.

"Well, off you go, Katie," he said. "Maybe you'll help me up next time when I fall."

Katie smiled at Stephen.

"You have a beautiful daughter," said Lila, wistfully. "You're very lucky."

"Thank you," answered Katie's mother.

"Holy macker...!"

Stephen and Lila quickly turned around at the sound of Nat's cry, fast enough to see his waving arms, shuffling feet, and subsequent fall to the ice. They sped to him.

"I'm o.k. kids," Nat mumbled, trying to force a smile as he looked up at them. "Just lost my footing. Give me a second."

"Take your time, Nat." said Stephen. "When you're ready I'll give you a hand."

"Thanks, pal." Nat took a deep breath. "O.K., ready when you are."

"Sorry to leave you alone," said Stephen, as he helped Nat to his feet.

"No need to apologize. Gotta help the little kid. I survived. Funny thing, though. First time I was even aware of somebody else on the ice besides us. So wrapped up in just keepin' on my feet, didn't even notice all the other people skatin'. Started lookin' around and bang, lost my balance and the rest is history. Good thing you two got your wits about you."

"Are you sure you're alright?" asked Lila, anxiously.

"None the worse for wear. Hips feel fine." Nat rubbed his bottom and grimaced. "Might have a bruise there, though."

"I wouldn't doubt it," said Lila.

"Maybe it's time to go," suggested Stephen.

"I'm beat," said Nat.

"How about something to eat?" asked Stephen.

"Wouldn't mind that," answered Nat. "How 'bout you Lila?"

"I'm ready for dinner. We've been skating a good while now."

They left the ice and once again entered the pavilion. After unlacing their skates and changing into their shoes, they left the park. They walked, three abreast with their skates slung over their shoulders. They walked in silence, all three tired from the afternoon's activity. Their silence gave Nat pause to think. His thoughts turned to Lila. He recalled the hesitancy in her answer when he asked in the restaurant how she and Stephen had been. He retrieved from his memory her sentence, "It's not always easy being an adult, either." The afternoon's image of a more lighthearted Lila enjoying herself contrasted with those recollections. Something didn't fit, thought Nat. Something, somewhere… He couldn't put his finger on it.

❄❄

Following a quick dinner at the restaurant, they set out for home. With a brisk wind at their backs, they hurried along. In little time they reached the intersection where their streets diverged.

"Call us during the week, Nat. Don't forget," Lila said.

"I won't forget," he responded. "Minds becomin' as sharp as a tack lately. Even remembered where I put my glasses this mornin'." He began to walk away.

"See you soon!" called Stephen.

"You got it!" shouted back Nat. He suddenly stopped. "Oops, did forget somethin'. Gotta give you back the skates you lent me. Maybe I'm not so sharp after all." He took a few steps into the wind while removing the skates from his shoulder. "Thanks," he said, the ice skates dangling from his outstretched hand.

"You're welcome," answered Stephen, taking them from him. "I'm glad my old skates weren't too large for you."

"A little big but did the trick anyhow. I'm glad you saved 'em. Never know what's gonna be. Maybe someday you'll be standin' in my shoes. Ever hear of ripple soles?" chuckled Nat.

"Vaguely", answered Stephen.

"How about bicycle riding in the spring?"

Nat and Stephen turned to Lila, incredulously.

"We have that old bike in the shed, Stephen," she continued. "What do you think, Nat?"

"Talkin' about old," shivered Nat, "the old man is gettin' cold."

Lila reached out and gently turned up the collar of Nat's coat. "There," she said, "we don't want you getting sick again. Bicycle riding can wait."

"Goodnight then... and thanks. Been quite a day." Nat turned to leave.

Stephen put his arm around Lila and they watched as Nat slowly walked away.

Lila leaned her head upon Stephen's shoulder. "I'm cold too," she sighed. "I wish winter would be over. Let's go home." They too started on their way.

"Haven't rode a bike in I don't know how long!" Nat's words, shouted into a nearly implacable wind, barely reached them from the end of the block. "But you got a date!"

"He's incorrigible," said Stephen.

Just Be Kind To Her, Nat

NAT STOOD, ILLUMINATED BY THE moon, and rummaged through his pockets in search of his keys.

"Sharp as a tack," he laughed aloud. "Now I can't even find my keys."

After finally locating them, he opened his front door and stepped inside. He took off his hat, scarf, and overcoat.

"Not as young as I used to be," he mumbled, dropping into his chair.

Alone in the darkness, half asleep, he contemplated his good fortune. Not in words, for his feelings had not yet crystallized into them. He simply sensed a change. It had taken these few encounters with Stephen and Lila for him to feel the extent of his solitude. With Ida's death he had become entombed in a labyrinth of sorrow, a maze of remembrance. He had sought no exit. Now, he had been shown the door to the present. It had swung open onto an ice skating rink. He had crossed the threshold of that doorway and had taken a few tentative steps back into life, even tried to glide back in. He had got a little ahead of himself and had fallen. He had picked himself up with a little help and once again had stood on his own two feet. He had crossed the border dividing solitude from companionship. The map that

gave him direction still evoked the past, though with it, he was
beginning to navigate the present.

❀❀

He dozed off in his chair, exhausted. Finally, sometime in the
night, he awakened and groped his way to the bedroom in the
dark. He undressed and fell into bed. In the depths of his sleep,
he dreamed of Ida. He awoke with a start, in his dream, from a
deep slumber, slouched in his armchair, fully clothed. There she
stood, right in front of him. He thought that he must be dreaming and that assuredly he had fallen asleep, as was his habit, in
his armchair late at night. He reached for his glasses, put them
on, and looked again. There she stood.

"So," she said, with a look of chagrin, "I should continue
to worry about you. You should be out ice skating and maybe
break your neck!"

Nat stared at her, tilting his head to the side in puzzlement.
My beautiful wife, he thought to himself, comes to me in the
middle of the night to talk about ice skating.

"But I'm gettin' good," he answered. "Did you see? Aside
from one fall, I'm doin' good."

"Maybe so," admitted Ida in return, "but better you should
take a nice walk or sit safe and read the paper."

"You're a worry wart," Nat teased her. "I wish you'd come
out and try it with me. Just like in the old days."

"Ach." She waved her hand at him and laughed. "Me on
skates. That would be a sight."

"What do you think of my friends, Ida? They're good people, yes?"

"A lucky thing, Nat. For so many days these last years I see you alone and my heart aches. You should enjoy good company still."

"They certainly are good, Ida. And Lila's soup!" Nat shook his head approvingly. "Just like yours. You wouldn't believe it."

"She's been kind to you, Nat. She's a lovely girl."

"I know, Ida. But there's something I can't figure out about her. Got her whole life ahead of her. A fine husband. Nice home. But I figure somethin' is eatin' at her. I was never as sharp as you when it came to people and I can't put my finger on this, but I got a feelin' something hurts her deeply."

A tear appeared in the corner of Ida's eye and trickled down her cheek.

"You're a good man, Nat. A good soul."

Nat smiled and tried to rise from his armchair. He wished to stand and embrace her. His body felt limp, exhausted. It would not respond to his heart's desire.

"Is there anything I can do for her?" he asked.

"Ach. I wish there were, Nat. I wish there were. Not even my chicken soup can cure what ails your friend. Just be kind to her, Nat. Just be kind."

Nat's eyelids grew heavy with fatigue. He could not keep Ida in focus. As he began to doze, he thought he could still hear her voice in the distance, slowly fading to a whisper.

"What is this I hear about a bicycle? You be careful, Nat. It's been a good forty years since..."

In a deep slumber, Nat stretched out his arm. It lay draped over the empty half of the bed.

The Forest For The Trees

By the middle of the week, winter had temporarily eased its cold grip. Wednesday dawned with abundant sunshine and unseasonable warmth. Mothers and their children emerged from indoors, responding to the call of an unexpected winter's treat.

Lila stood at the entrance to the playground. The gate was closed. It may as well have been locked shut, for all that she felt. On her way home from school she had stopped. The children dashed around the playground, from the swings, to the slide, to the see-saw. They played merrily, in joyful abandon.

Some women followed their toddlers around, pushed them on swings, or guided them up the slide and caught them coming down. Others sat on benches, rocking children in strollers, smiling at their babies, and conversing with one another. Lila watched in silence, wishing to leave, yet unable to move. She yearned to push open the gate with a child in tow, her child. She hungered to be on the other side of the fence, running across the playground in pursuit of a child, her child.

Not far from Lila, partially hidden behind a tree, stood Nat. He had been out for a walk. Not for a newspaper or a meal, but simply to stroll. He had come upon her quite by accident while in the process of aimlessly traversing one street after another. When the vague outline of a woman at the park gate turned into Lila, he was initially inclined to approach and say hello. Why he did not do so, mystified him. For instead of approaching her, he stopped beside a tree and stepped behind it, shielding himself from her. Something about her demeanor had halted him in his tracks. She had always appeared to him so warm and expressive, inviting him to return her openness in kind. And now she stood, alone, expressing something altogether different. Nat could sense it in the rigidity of her posture and the riveting look with which she surveyed the playground. Her solitary figure seemed to preclude any intrusion. He could only see one side of her face, and even that, not too clearly. Peering from behind the tree, he could discern a tautness in her countenance, unlike the soft, welcoming visage he had come to know. He gazed from Lila to the children and back again. He thought for a few moments. Images of her and Stephen flashed through his mind. Some of the things she had said came to mind. He remembered his nap in their living room and thinking that there was no sign of kids around the house. Again, he looked from Lila to the children. Then, with great solemnity, he shook his head from side to side.

"Now I understand," he mumbled to himself.

Though he could not know her exact circumstances, he was able to surmise the nature of her anguish. How, he wondered, could he have been so blind. Ida, she'd a known right away. She'd a taken Lila under her wing and cheered her up alright. Would've talked to her. Maybe given her good advice. But not old Nat. Not me. Can't see the forest for the trees sometimes. Geez. Poor kid. Tough for a young kid.

He leaned against the tree, his eyes still fixed upon her, his head filled with thoughts and reproaches.

Too wrapped up in myself, he thought. Too much sittin' around feelin' bad about myself. Shoulda been more aware. Picked up something but just didn't put two and two together.

He continued to watch her. He considered turning around and walking in a different direction. He thought of crossing to the other side of the street and continuing on, perhaps unnoticed. He did not wish to disturb her. He did not want to let her know that he had seen her. But, it was too late. She suddenly turned in his direction, perhaps sensing someone's presence, and gazed towards him. She took a few steps along the fence, edging closer. He became flustered, the blood rushing to his face in embarrassment.

"Nat, is that you?"

"Um, well..." his voice faltered.

"How long have you been there? Are you alright?"

"Just, um, just fine. Walking home as a matter of fact." He attempted to gain his composure.

"It's a beautiful day. Don't you agree?" Lila smiled at him, her longing hidden behind a cheerful greeting.

"How's Stephen?" he mumbled.

"Just fine, Nat."

"And you. How have you been?"

She glanced towards the playground. He noticed and said nothing.

"Can I walk you home?" she offered.

He turned up his collar and shoved each of his hands into a coat pocket. Lila, now standing beside him, nonchalantly slid her right arm around his left elbow. They walked along. As they passed the closed gate, Lila stole one last glimpse of the children playing and just as quickly turned her attention to Nat.

"Roast chicken for dinner tonight, Nat? I couldn't entice you into some fresh fish?"

He returned a weak smile. He did not want to talk about food or ice skating or anything else for that matter. He just wanted to say something to Lila that would truly cheer her up. He wanted to say something that would make a difference in her life. He wanted to do something for her.

"You know," he began, "when Ida took sick the bottom just fell right out. I didn't know what to do. She was in such pain and the doctors said it would be bad. Real bad. Some days I just sat and cried. Couldn't take watchin' her suffer. Couldn't stand the thought of losin' her, of bein' without her."

He stopped talking, staring straight ahead, his eyes watery, his features contorted. Lila looked at the side of his face but did not speak. He was marshalling all of his will to keep those painful memories from undermining his desire to continue.

"It... it killed me to see..." he said, "and just the thought of it now. Even after so long. It still..."

He stopped again.

This will not do, he thought to himself. I wanted to cheer her up. I wanted to do something for her and here I am blubbering about my own sorrows. I wanted to make a point and I know what it was and it's not coming out right. Not at all.

Lila was about to speak when he drew a deep breath and started up again.

"So, to make a long story short… I never thought that I would ever feel good again. I never thought that I would ever smile again." He drew in another deep breath and continued with a new found tone of authority. "I never thought I'd feel any different than the day I buried my Ida. It was over for me too. I couldn't see anything ahead for me. No joys. No consolation. No nothin'. And now, may my Ida rest in peace, I smile a little bit and maybe I ice skate a little and fall on my behind. Maybe there's a little hope for me. Maybe I'll be a little like the 'old' Nat. Not just old Nat. Maybe. Maybe not. You never know."

He sighed, then smiled broadly. He had finished. He had crossed a bridge whose span led from sorrow and self-pity to the other side, to life. It was a bridge constructed of words, words affirming life. Only to cross it you had to speak those words, or moreso, hear yourself speak them. He heard himself very clearly and was astounded at what he heard.

Lila heard him clearly as well and knew that he had certainly seen her at the park gate and understood that she too harbored her own private sorrow. She knew that her longing for a child had been all too clear to Nat's eyes. And now the bond between them had become all too clear to her. Though years and worlds apart from one another, Lila realized just how much a bond of sorrow and loneliness connected her and Nat. How ironic she thought to herself, an old man longing for a past he cannot regain and a young woman, longing for a future she seemingly cannot possess. How hard it must have been for him to say what he said, she thought. How hard must it have been to unearth his pain and put it in words to cheer her.

"Thank you, Nat," she whispered. "I know that wasn't easy for you to say."

"I should be thanking you," he answered.

Another Kind Of Loneliness

THERE ARE LIMITS TO WHAT one can deduce from behind a tree. If Nat ever thought he had cornered the market on loneliness, he'd have been surprised to learn just how wide a market it truly is. Lila too possessed her little corner. Though he could not always fully comprehend the depth of her loneliness, Stephen shared that corner with Lila, as he shared everything with her. Their life together, once bright and cheerful, had for the past few years taken on a patina of gray. Disappointment and dashed hopes had reined in their expectations and dampened their once sunny outlook. If Nat could have stood behind that same tree four years before and spied Lila at the gate to the park, he'd have seen a different Lila and perhaps reached a different conclusion. He would have seen a smiling face enjoying a scene that she assumed would one day include her and her own son or daughter.

❋❋

It was in another lifetime that Lila and Stephen possessed a clear vision of the future, a limitless horizon without a dark cloud in sight. It was a time of autumn drives and camping out beside an open fire on a summer's night. It was a time of bicycle rides, walks in the rain, and angels in the snow. They could see no obstacles ahead to the fulfillment of their heart's desire, the greatest being to one day have children together. Mornings then found Lila awakening refreshed each day and eager to go to work. Stephen awakened each day with a sense that his world was in order. Their conversations then often revolved around weekend plans, their latest household project, or daily events at work. They lived in a self sustaining bubble that simply floated along, fueled by their love for one another and buoyed by youthful optimism. They could not foresee anything straight ahead or around the next bend that would derail them from the track they were on. They were two halves forming a whole. Lila possessed an intuitive understanding of the entanglements of the heart, complemented by Stephen's practical nature. They often found it amusing, how different they could be from one another. Yet, the irony of how their divergent natures continually blended together to make their life so enjoyable, was not lost upon them. They appreciated what they had together and wanted something more.

Having already established a household and fairly secure careers, they surmised that the next step would be the simplest, letting nature take its course. It was under a star filled sky on a summer night, beside Swinging Bridge Lake, in that other lifetime, that Stephen saw more than the glow of the campfire's flames dancing in Lila's eyes.

"Come, let's go," she said, reaching for his hand.

"Let me put out the fire first," he responded, reaching for a stick to disperse the fire's embers.

"Just leave it," laughed Lila, grabbing his hand. "It will burn out by itself."

Stephen glanced at the orange flames, then into Lila's eyes. "You're right."

Lila led him into the tent. They undressed, shivering in the late August air, enveloped in darkness but for the light cast by the last flickering flames of the campfire.

"Warm me up," whispered Lila, as they slipped beneath the heavy blankets.

She closed her eyes and felt Stephen's arms encircle her, felt the warm, secure embrace she had come to know and rely on.

"I love you, Lila," he whispered back.

They drifted away together to the sound of their own breathing and the crackling of the fire's last glowing embers.

As the sun ascended in the sky the next morning, light gradually filtered into the tent. Stephen opened his eyes and looked at Lila, peacefully sleeping beside him. The filtered sunlight washed across her face, casting a soft morning's haze upon her features. Stephen stared at her long eyelashes and the errant strands of long hair that fell across her face. He knew that he would never tire of looking at that face, that it held for him that morning as much enchantment as it did the day they met.

Lila opened her eyes.

"You're staring at me," she yawned, propping herself up on her elbow.

"Only for a little while," said Stephen.

"I like when you stare at me." She yawned again. "Tell me what you see."

"I see the only person I would ever want to be with. I see the one person I can never imagine being without."

Lila brushed the hair away from her face and shivered, pulling the blanket up to her chin.

"Sometimes I get scared, Stephen. We've known each other forever. Sometimes it crosses my mind, what if something happens to one of us? What then? I don't know what I would do without you. And what if you were alone? What if something happened to me?"

Stephen reached out and gently touched her lips with his forefinger.

"Shh...," he whispered. "Don't Lila. Don't ever think..."

A tear appeared in her eye.

"You're so sensitive," he smiled. "You're such a strong person. So strong and sometimes you just...just melt. I've lost count of how many tears I've wiped from your eyes since we've been together."

"You're making fun of me now. Aren't you, Stephen?" She smiled back at him.

"Any chance I can," he answered with a wide grin.

Lila didn't hesitate. She quickly rolled over on top of him and kissed him, pulling the blanket over both their heads.

❄❄

Not long after that morning, the bubble burst. Their youthful optimism was no match for an ageless adversary, mother nature. Six months of trying to get pregnant without success led to puzzlement. Another six months led to frustration, fear, and uncertainty.

The peaceful, contented face that Stephen stared at that morning in the tent was beginning to disappear. The face that Nat saw from behind the tree, taut and strained, had begun to evolve over the course of that year.

As that year passed and with another August upon them, Lila knew it was time to seek help.

"I'm sorry, Stephen," she said through a cascade of uncontrollable tears, early one Sunday morning.

"Why are you apologizing?" Stephen reached for her.

"I wanted so much to be pregnant this year. I wanted to start a family. I'm just so... frustrated." Her voice faltered as her body tensed and she clenched her fists, drawing a deep breath.

"Lila, please don't... It'll happen."

"But something is wrong, Stephen. It must be."

"I'll do anything you want, Lila. You know that. Just tell me what you have in mind, what you think is best."

"I'm not sure myself, Stephen." Lila paused, wiped the tears from her face, and continued. "A year of trying is long enough. I'm sorry, Stephen. I never thought we would end up here. I'm ready for a baby. I'm ready to be a mother. It's so frustrating to be emotionally prepared for something and then not have it happen. I guess I took it for granted that just because we were ready for the next step that it would simply happen."

"We'll figure it out, Lila," said Stephen firmly. "I know we will. There's...there's a solution to everything."

"I hope we can. It's just that time goes by so quickly and now is the right time for us. It will only get harder as we get older. We've had such a good time together all these years. We waited to have children and now I hope we didn't wait too long."

Knowing so well her love for children and what a good mother she would be, it pained Stephen to hear the frustration and disappointment so clearly evident in Lila's words. He wondered how such a simple and natural desire could turn into something so difficult and painful. He put his arms around her and drew her closer in a reassuring embrace.

She slipped from his embrace and took a step back, her disappointment suddenly transformed into anger. Her jaw tightened, her beauty momentarily set in stone. "We must see a doctor, Stephen," she said, in a voice imbued with urgency. "It's not enough to keep trying. Not after a year."

Stephen recoiled, his body stiffened as he grimaced.

Lila's features softened, as did her voice, for she immediately grasped Stephen's reaction. "Tell me what you think. It's not just up to me. We've always decided things together. Do you agree with me?"

"If it's what you want," Stephen offered, unconvincingly.

"But it's not what I want. It's what we have to do. You know me better than that, Stephen. We've only ever confided in each other. I know we've talked about this. I know how strongly you feel about keeping our private life just that, private. I don't disagree with you. When the girls at..."

"But Lila, what if..." Stephen began.

"Wait, Stephen, let me finish my thought," she interrupted.

She caught her breath and continued.

"When the girls at school talk about their personal life I just listen. I don't feel comfortable joining in. I know we feel the same way about that. We've all become voyeurs. Every personal detail about everyone's life is out there for the asking today. I've always loved feeling that all of my secrets are safe with you. Once we see a doctor we will be opening the door to the most intimate part of our life. I don't know what will happen after we walk through that door, but we have to agree to walk through together." She paused momentarily. "Now tell me what you think."

Stephen looked at her intently. He admired her resolve to confront her disappointment and move forward. He looked into her heart and saw her maternal instinct held in abeyance by something she could not grasp. He weighed that against his instinct, to keep trying on their own and not open up their private life to anyone. He was constantly making decisions at the bank, sitting at his desk, weighing choices in a methodical, deliberative manner and then making firm, clear decisions. He was relied on to do so. Only now he wasn't looking at a balance sheet or sitting across from a client. He wasn't studying numbers or reviewing figures. It was a different kind of balance that he sought now. This, after all, was about Lila.

"We'll do whatever we have to," he said, his voice steady and resolute.

"Are you sure? I don't know what the problem is, Stephen, or what we may have to do. There may not be a simple solution."

"I understand."

❀❀

Lila sat pensively, her strained features further approaching what Nat would come to see a few years hence, so unlike the glow encompassing Maggie's face. Maggie was just unwrapping the last gift of the baby shower, the gift that Lila had given her. Lila didn't want to be there, or anywhere, that the joy of childbirth was being celebrated. It was just too painful for her.

Another year of trying had passed, another fruitless year of trying. Only this year had brought with it, for her and Stephen, medical exams and tests, medications, confusion and apprehension. It had been an unkind year. It had finally culminated in a miscarriage.

"I love it," exclaimed Maggie. She held up the small, colorful patchwork blanket.

"I...I'm so glad," responded Lila, startled from her momentary reverie.

"It's beautiful, Lila. Thank you so much."

Lila collected herself as Maggie struggled to rise from the soft cushioned armchair she had sunk so deeply into.

"No, don't get up, Maggie," said Lila.

"It's perfectly alright," answered Maggie. "I'm so uncomfortable. Sitting. Standing. I'd just as soon get up and move a little bit."

She edged her way to Lila, around the new high chair that sat between them and then alongside the narrow coffee table.

"You're a sweetheart," she whispered, hugging Lila.

"It is beautiful, Lila," joined Sandy. "Did you make it yourself?"

"Yes," Lila whispered.

"Please make one for me when I have a baby. Would you?"

"I'd love one also," chimed in Amy.

The women filled the small living room with laughter.

"You all better hurry up then," quipped Maggie, giggling. "Put your orders in soon while Lila's still available. Who knows when we'll be having a shower for her?"

Lila sat motionless with Maggie now beside her on the couch. She suddenly felt uncomfortably warm, though it was a seasonable autumn day and the windows in the room were partially open. She began to perspire. Maggie's last sentence echoed in her mind as the women chatted all around her. Gripped by a mixture of overwhelming anxiety and sadness, she felt her stomach churning and sensed the dampness of her body beneath her sweater. She sat very still, though in her mind's eye she could clearly see herself running from the room. Of course, she thought to herself, Maggie did not mean any harm by her words. How could Maggie know? How could anyone know what she was experiencing and how she felt? Was it too much to ask? Too much to want? Why couldn't she be opening baby gifts? Why couldn't she be filled with joy and anticipation at this point in her life instead of sitting with her friends while feeling so alone?

"Lila?"

Lila turned in Maggie's direction.

"Lila, are you alright?" Maggie asked. "You look a little flush."

"I'm fine," answered Lila timidly, her response lacking conviction.

"Oh, my. The baby is kicking again. Here, give me your hand." Maggie reached for Lila's hand. "Your palm is moist, Lila. You're sweating. Are you sure you're alright?"

"I'm fine, Maggie. Don't worry."

Lila placed her hand on Maggie's stomach, waited a moment and then felt the little tap on her palm.

Maggie beamed. "Did you feel it?" she asked.

"Absolutely," answered Lila, trying to sound enthusiastic while mustering a faint smile.

She tried so hard to share Maggie's pleasure. A baby shower was always on the horizon these days, or so it seemed to her. She tried mightily to evoke joy on these occasions only to end up not just feeling bad for herself, but also guilty for not fully appreciating a friend's happiness. Soon, she suspected, she would demure from going to them at all.

Tea and coffee were served shortly. Lila felt a sense of relief as the afternoon came to a close. She would at least be able to escape from that room, if not from her thoughts.

❈❈

"The glass is half full," insisted Stephen, grasping for something positive to say. "It will get better."

"It's all I think about. I've become obsessive. I know I have. I wish I could stop. I save all of my sorrow for you. Am I wearing you down? Making you miserable?"

"No. I just wish you weren't so sad all the time."

It was five thirty in the morning and they were sitting across from one another at the kitchen table. Between them were two cups of hot coffee and a rich history to warm them. It was not enough to ward off the night's waning chill.

Lila had awakened first. She had awakened with a start after another sleepless night.

It was beginning to happen often, usually following the same pattern. Her eyes would suddenly open and there she would find herself, staring into the darkness at nothing. She would lie mute in bed, not wishing to awaken Stephen, while a voice inside of her would scream out in anguish and frustration. She lamented the life that she did not lead with the child that she could not have as the tears ran down her cheeks at three in the morning. Three turned to four and four to five. She barely moved. She did not want to wake Stephen. She did not even want to be awake, herself. "If only I could get back to sleep," she would think to herself. "Just to get back to sleep and not feel so depleted in the morning." Contrary to her wishes, she never could get back to sleep. She would get up and wander to the kitchen. Stephen would soon follow, having sensed her absence from beside him in bed.

"I'm sorry, Stephen. I just get overwhelmed sometimes."

"I know you do. I just don't always know what I can do for you."

"You're doing all you can. I've asked a lot of you and you never let me down. I just can't find any balance with this. I can't put it in any perspective. I feel so guilty sometimes. Maybe I don't appreciate what I do have. Maybe I'm just selfish. Am I wrong?"

"No, there's nothing wrong with what you want. There's nothing wrong with wanting to have a baby."

"When will it end, Stephen?" asked Lila, plaintively.

"I don't know, Lila. It just doesn't add up."

"Not everything does, Stephen!" she retorted.

"Lila!"

"I'm so sorry, Stephen. It's just been so… stressful. I'm so frustrated."

Stephen let her comment go.

Lila could see in his forgiving eyes that her hurtful words did not linger.

"But that's just it, Stephen," she continued "It all seems so random. I know this is not uncommon, but why us? Why?"

"It is random," agreed Stephen. "But… I think it's alright," he added, soothingly.

Lila looked at him, puzzled. He continued.

"Random things happen. Unexpected things happen. They never happened to us. At least not until now. I kept trying to figure this out. I kept asking the same thing. Why? I couldn't find an answer, just like you. For the first time in my life I couldn't come up with a solution. And then I realized, maybe there is no answer. Maybe there isn't an apparent reason for everything. Random things are just a part of life, anybody's life. They come along in one form or another and we simply have to accept them and deal with them the best we can. And that's what we're doing, Lila. The doctor said it would be a long haul. He hasn't given up hope and neither will we."

Lila reached across the table and took Stephen's hand.

"I'll try and be more positive, Stephen. I always feel better after we talk about this."

"Just be yourself, Lila," said Stephen, beseechingly.

"I'm not so sure who that is anymore."

Stephen squeezed her hand.

❦❦

Lila tried to remain positive. Stephen held tight to a glass half full. As time went on, the word why disappeared from their lips, to be replaced by when. Lila had a second miscarriage. More tests and procedures followed. It was hard for either of them to maintain their optimism as they navigated a sea of modern technology with no guarantee of reaching shore with a child in tow. Time continued to pass.

❦❦

So it was on that late winter's afternoon that Nat saw a solitary young woman standing at the gate to the park and recognized the face of another kind of loneliness. It was a loneliness usually well hidden from the world that took a certain sensibility to see. It could be seen through the eyes of an old man to whom loneliness was no stranger.

There Is A Season

"*I*'M LATE."

Stephen fixed his eyes on Lila for an instant and then quickly glanced at his watch.

"No, silly," she grinned. "I'm late."

"Oh," he responded calmly. Hesitating a moment, he put two and two together and exclaimed, "Oh!" He reached across the dinner table and took Lila's hand while looking into her clear blue eyes. "How long?" he asked.

"It's been a week, Stephen. I didn't want to say anything sooner. I guess I was scared and didn't want to disappoint either of us. I don't want to get my hopes up too high."

"I love you, Lila. I'm just, just...I mean...how?"

"We both know how," giggled Lila.

"That's not what I meant," smiled Stephen.

"I know you didn't," responded Lila, smiling back at him. "I just couldn't resist. That could be the first time that I've ever seen you get flustered. But I guess there's been a lot of firsts with this for both of us." Lila sighed. "Maybe it's because we slowed things down and stopped trying so hard. It's been about six months since we stopped with the doctors. Maybe trying to relax a little and have a normal life, whatever that is, helped. Like everything else, nothing is completely clear."

"Wouldn't that be something, Lila, if that's what it is. After all we've been through, if things just happened naturally, anyway. But you know what? It doesn't matter now. Here we are. Still standing!"

"I'm going to go over to the lab after work tomorrow to have a blood test. I'm not sure what time I'll be home."

"So you'll be late again tomorrow," Stephen smiled.

Lila laughed at his little joke.

"It's nice to see you laugh," said Stephen. "Seeing you laughing and ice skating..."

"Oh, my goodness!" exclaimed Lila. "I forgot to tell you what happened this afternoon. I met Nat on my way home. My mind was so preoccupied, I forgot to tell you."

"Where?"

"Near the park. He was out for a walk."

"How is he?"

"Actually," replied Lila, "he's a little sore. He said his legs ache a little bit and he's got a little bruise on his..."

"I know," Stephen interjected, "from the fall."

Lila shook her head and continued.

"We talked for a while. He's such a sweetheart. When I said that spring would soon be here and I mentioned our garden, his eyes lit up. It seems he had a garden of his own but stopped gardening after Ida died. I promised him we'd come over and take a look at his yard, Stephen, and help him get his garden started again. He was so excited. I hope you don't mind. I promised him we'd be there Saturday morning."

"I don't mind at all. But, no gardening for you. You're going to just sit and watch. Will you promise me that?"

"I will."

"Let's keep our fingers crossed. No matter what happens, we'll deal with it."

He let go of her hand and stood up, a dish in his hand.

"I guess we should clear the table," he said.

Lila took the plate from his hand and put it back on the table.

"Hold me first," she whispered.

Stephen embraced her tightly and felt the gentle movement of her body, pressed against his, as she softly sobbed.

✳✳

As Stephen turned the corner, he could see Nat waving to him in the distance. He pulled the car alongside the curb as Nat bounded out into the street to greet him. Nat was standing beside the driver's side window before Stephen had even opened the car door.

"So where's the little lady?" asked Nat, peering into the car window.

Stephen opened the door.

"What's that you said, Nat?"

"I was wondering where your lovely wife is."

"Oh. She was a little tired this morning, Nat. She stayed in bed but said to tell you that if she feels up to it she'll walk over a little later. She's also waiting for a phone call this morning, so she may be a while."

"It is kinda early, I guess. Really shouldn't be draggin' you kids outa bed at this hour of the morning. Two of you work so hard all week."

"It's alright, Nat. Spring is just around the corner and rumor has it you're some gardener. The sooner we get started the better."

"Who's startin' rumors like that?" Nat asked with a wink.

"The little lady," smiled Stephen.

Nat threw his arm around Stephen's shoulder.

"Come on, pal. I'll show you the yard. It's not a pretty sight."

"Don't worry, Nat. We'll do the best we can. Just give me a second. I brought some garden tools with me. Lila even had me pick up some seeds and fertilizer this week. Just in case we get that far. They're in the trunk."

"Let me give you a hand," offered Nat.

Stephen reached into the trunk and handed Nat the box of gardening tools. He grabbed the heavy bag of fertilizer and the packets of seed.

"Lead the way, Nat," he said, closing the trunk.

They walked single file along a narrow path adjacent to the side of the house and stopped at a rusted metal gate. Nat jiggled the latch and with a modicum of force, pushed against the gate. It creaked open, brushing back a thick carpet of weeds.

"Maybe this isn't such a good idea," he frowned, turning to Stephen.

"You just lead the way," replied Stephen.

The weeds reached to their knees. As they walked in single file across the yard, Stephen glanced to either side. To his left he noticed a small patio, bare but for an old rusted wrought iron table and two rusted chairs. To his right, sticking up above the grass, was the handle of what appeared to be a lawn mower. Stephen took a few steps in its direction, kneeled down and parted the weeds.

"Gee, Nat. This is an old push lawnmower. How long have you had it?"

"Don't remember," replied Nat. "Might be an original."

"I'll bet we could get it going again," said Stephen, examining the mower. "Just a little oil here and there and who knows. Bring it right back to life."

Stephen stood up and rejoined Nat. After a few more steps together, they came to a standstill. They both looked down and surveyed the rectangular outline of what was once Nat's garden.

"Worse than I thought," muttered Nat.

"We sure have our work cut out for us," replied Stephen. "But we'll get it done, Nat," he added encouragingly.

"Gotta a plan, Stephen?"

"Well, why don't we frame out the original garden first. I brought some hand trowels and I'm sure you have a shovel. Then we can clear the weeds. After that, if you've got a pitchfork, we can start turning over the soil and mix in the fertilizer."

"It's a plan, buddy," Nat nodded in agreement. "Still a little sore from skatin', but I'm game."

They gardened side by side. They conversed and worked for short stretches of time in silence. Their camaraderie seemed to dispel their difference in age. Weeks before this day, before they found themselves laboring together in Nat's yard, they had planted the kind of seeds that do not come in a tiny packet, seeds of friendship. Without a cloud on the horizon, the early morning sun cast its light upon the growing friendship taking shape in Nat's garden.

"I'm gettin' done in," sighed Nat, taking a deep breath and wiping his brow with his forearm. "How 'bout a breather?"

"Sounds good to me," exclaimed Stephen. He looked at his watch. "I guess we've been going at it for almost two hours."

"How 'bout a cold glass of water, pal? Tell you what. You have a seat over on the patio and I'll go inside and hustle us up two glasses of water."

Nat entered the house through a back door as Stephen sat down in one of the rusted patio chairs. No sooner had he sat down, than he heard the creak of the backyard gate swinging open.

"Stephen?"

He heard Lila's familiar voice.

"Over here," he answered. From where he sat he could see the broad smile that graced her lips and discern the joy in her eyes. He stood up as she approached, his arms opened wide. He knew immediately.

Lila nodded.

Stephen embraced her and held her tightly. Releasing her, he took a step back and gazed into her eyes.

Just then Nat stepped out of the house with a glass of water in each hand.

"Ah, your lovely wife!" he exclaimed, seeing Lila.

He walked to the table and put the glasses down.

Suddenly, tears began to run down Stephen's cheeks. He dropped to the chair, crying. His body gently shook as he sobbed uncontrollably.

Lila knelt in front of him and put her hands on his knees.

"What is it, Stephen?" she implored.

Her blue eyes glowed. Her entire face was an open invitation sent lovingly to his heart, seeking its confidence.

"I'm sorry, Lila. I..."

"Don't apologize, Stephen," she answered softly. "You're allowed to cry."

"I never do," sobbed Stephen, shaking his head.

"I know you don't." Lila gently touched his face and wiped away his tears.

"I think I'm just overwhelmed, Lila. It's all been sitting inside. It's been so long and here we are again. I'm so happy and... and I'm scared. What if we lose..."

"Shh...Stephen." Lila had placed her forefinger across his lips before he could finish his sentence. "Now it's my turn, Stephen. Everything will be fine. I promise."

Stephen's tears subsided.

He took Lila's hands in his and gently pulled her up, guiding her onto his lap. They sat quietly together, momentarily oblivious to their surroundings.

While they were speaking to one another, Nat had stood by the table in silence. Listening to their conversation and seeing their faces, he had surmised just exactly what was transpiring. Gettin' better at figurin' things out. Ida'd be proud of me, he thought to himself. Overcome with joy at the news, he could no longer contain himself.

"Got yourselves a babysitter right here!" he blurted out.

Stephen and Lila turned in his direction.

"Oops," said Nat, turning red and covering his mouth with his hand.

Stephen and Lila broke into laughter.

Nat joined them.

"Brought you that glass of water," he said, catching his breath. "Here, Lila, you take the other glass." He grabbed the glasses of water and offered one to each of them.

"Thank you, Nat," they said in unison.

"Just plain water. Nothin' special in it like Lila's tea." He grinned.

"That's alright, Nat," said Stephen. "It's still morning."

"Some break this is," smiled Nat. "Too much excitement for an old man. What d'ya say we knock off and you two go out and celebrate. Finish this another time."

"A promise is a promise," said Lila.

"That's true, Nat," Stephen agreed. "Besides, we'll have plenty of time to celebrate."

He winked at Lila. "Now, let's get that garden up and running."

After Lila rose from his lap, Stephen stood up and gently guided her into the chair.

"You sit down and rest. You promised you would. No work for you. Just relax and enjoy the sun."

"I will."

❅❆

Stephen and Nat returned to work. Nat pulled more weeds while Stephen started turning the earth that had already been cleared.

"So you think we're gonna have a garden here?" asked Nat, looking over in Stephen's direction from his hands and knees.

"You just wait and see," answered Stephen. "By the end of the summer we're going to have more tomatoes than we'll know what to do with."

"Used to grow the best tomatoes around, Stephen. Boy, do I remember that!"

"I remember, Nat, one year Lila and I grew so many we were eating tomato sauce all winter. Lila had all the burners going that fall. She must have been boiling up tomato sauce in every pot we owned. She literally filled the freezer with containers of sauce. There wasn't room for anything else. Never mind if you were looking for an ice cube."

Nat smiled.

"Had a freezer like that myself," he laughed, "only it wasn't filled with tomato sauce. Ever seen a freezer filled with pot roast?"

"I can't say that I have, Nat."

"Well, leave it to Ida, bless her soul. Up at five o'clock in the morning most days. Cookin' up pot roasts before she even went to work. Used to freeze 'em in containers. Line 'em up on the table. Enough in each for one dinner. Freezer full of 'em. Ate a lot of pot roast. That's for sure. Stephen, she was some cook."

"I'll bet she was. If that chicken soup was any indication..."

"Tip of the iceberg. Just the tip of the iceberg. If you coulda tasted all the stuff she could make. Especially on holidays."

Nat's eyes lit up. He dropped the clump of weeds that was in his grasp.

"Meatballs!" he exclaimed. "Do you like meatballs, Stephen?"

"Sure do," laughed Stephen.

"Well, Ida made these sweet and sour meatballs. Only on holidays mind you. Couldn't ever tell what she put in 'em. Never did ask. But who cared. They were unbelievable. I'm tellin' ya, Stephen. They came right after the soup on holidays. Soup then meatballs. She put a couple in a bowl for you. But you had to wait and finish the soup to get those meatballs. Kids could hardly wait. Me neither. I always tried sneakin' in the kitchen before company got there. Figured I could swipe a few from the pot while Ida wasn't there. Go figure, Stephen. She always knew. No matter where she was in the house, I can still here her yell. 'Nat, get away from that pot. Put down the spoon and get out of the kitchen. You wait.' Like she had eyes everywhere."

Nat paused. His eye had begun to tear and he rubbed it with the knuckle of his forefinger. "A little dirt musta gotten into it," he said. He blinked a few times.

"Are you alright?" asked Stephen.

"Guess so," answered Nat. "You know," he continued, "come to think of it, I can't remember ever seein' Ida with a cookbook or any kind of sheet of paper with a recipe on it. There were cookbooks sittin' right on top of the kitchen cabinets. Sittin' there right now. Never saw her open one. Musta all been in her head. Some things I can remember how to make from watchin' her. Like the soup. But those meatballs. I just don't know."

"Are you sure she didn't have a box with recipes in it, somewhere?" asked Lila.

She had been listening to the conversation with her eyes closed, resting in the glow of the late morning sun.

"Maybe she kept a file of recipes," she added. "In a kitchen drawer or cabinet."

Nat scratched his head.

"Hmm, gotta think about that one," he mused. "Maybe she did. A box with her mother's recipes. Could be. Cooked just like her mother. Had all these recipes swimmin' around in her head, but maybe they are written somewhere. Gotta look into that."

"It's just an idea, Nat," continued Lila, "but if Ida had some things written down, then we could cook up all kinds of things."

"And not eat so much roast chicken?" asked Nat, quizzically.

"That might be tough," answered Stephen, "but you'd survive."

"You're right, Stephen," Nat laughed. "It's worth a look see. Boy, I'd kill for a sweet and sour meatball."

He shook his head from side to side, slowly.

"Listen to me, will ya! Once I was a young fella with the whole world in front of me. Had big dreams then. Big dreams. And now. Now I'd just settle for a meatball. One simple meatball. What a world!"

"Not just any meatball," said Stephen.

"No, not just any meatball," sighed Nat. "You know what? I'm gonna do it! I'm gonna search around for those recipes and if I find 'em I'm gonna cook up some of those meatballs for all of us. That's a promise!"

Nat looked up towards the sky. He winked and waved his forefinger over his head.

"You're a smart one, you are."

They all looked up.

❄❄

"Runnin' outa steam," puffed Nat. "Gonna have to pull up a chair next to Lila in a minute."

The sun had reached its zenith as afternoon stretched before them.

"Gettin' a little hungry besides," he continued. "Must be all that talk about meatballs."

"Come sit by me," urged Lila. "I completely forgot that I brought lunch. It's in a knapsack by the fence. I dropped it when I came in the gate and heard Stephen's voice."

"I'll get it," offered Stephen. "Go sit and relax, Nat. Have a little something to eat with Lila. I'm going to keep working. I had a big breakfast."

"Don't mind if I do, buddy. Just a few minutes is all." Nat wiped the sweat from his brow with his forearm and walked over to the patio.

"Somethin' to be said for buyin' vegetables at the market," he smiled at Lila.

She smiled back.

Stephen retrieved the knapsack and pulled the other rusted chair over for Nat.

Nat and Lila sat beside one another, each nibbling on a half a sandwich. They exchanged gardening stories, from the joys of having a burgeoning crop of cucumbers to the disappointments of a failed corn crop.

Shortly, Nat rejoined Stephen. They worked side by side continuously, until Stephen thrust his shovel into the ground, leaned against its handle, and sighed.

"Well, the toughest part is done," he said, sighing once again. "Everything's been cleared and the dirt is all turned."

"You worked awful hard," responded Nat. "How 'bout a rest for you now?"

"Just a drink of water, Nat. I want to keep going. Lila was right. We can get some seeds in the ground today. Peas at least. They're an early crop. What do you think, Lila?" Stephen had turned in her direction.

"It's up to you. You must be exhausted."

"No, I can keep going. We have a little more time until dusk. I'm going to sprinkle the fertilizer across the garden. Then we'll rake it in and smooth it all out. What do you say, Nat?"

"I'm game."

Stephen grinned.

"You've been nothing but since the day we met you."

"Wonderin' what's next myself," mused Nat.

"Next we plant," answered Stephen. "How about it? It's all yours."

"Thanks, pal. How 'bout I make the holes for the seeds and Lila drops 'em in. Then you can cover each one up. We're a team aren't we?"

"I like that idea," said Lila, rising from her chair and looking radiant in the remaining glow of the slowly setting sun.

Lila walked over to the two of them. Stephen grabbed a packet of pea seeds from beside the box of gardening tools and handed it to Nat.

"Here Nat. It's all yours."

Nat tore open the packet and turned to Lila.

"Here you go, kid. Open your hand."

Nat poured out a handful of seeds.

"Let's do it!" he said, excitedly.

They planted three rows of peas. Then stepping back and standing abreast of one another, they contemplated their handiwork.

"I can't believe how much the two of you did," offered Lila, approvingly.

"Like I said. We're a team. All three of us," Nat beamed.

"What about watering?" asked Stephen.

"Got that covered," returned Nat. "Got a watering system that works like a charm. Set it up first thing tomorrow mornin'. You two take a break. You must be done in, Stephen. Don't know how I can ever repay the two of you for all you've done for me."

"How about the first tomato?" suggested Stephen.

Nat smiled from ear to ear and threw his arms around them both.

"It's yours!" he exclaimed.

With Nat's help, Stephen packed up all of the gardening tools he had brought along.

Nat walked them both to the car and as Stephen put everything into the trunk, Nat opened the passenger door for Lila.

"Goodbye, Nat." she said. "Get some rest."

Nat hesitated for a moment and then gently took her soft, smooth hand in his coarse, dirt stained one. He blushed and said, "Congratulations, Lila. I'm so happy for you." He kissed her on the cheek.

"Thank you, Nat," she whispered.

She got into the car and Nat closed the door.

"So... no more ice skating? I shouldn't have to worry about you anymore? One day it's ice skates and the next week it's peas. You should stick with peas. It's safer!"

Ida pointed a solitary finger at Nat as she half-heartedly admonished him.

Exhausted, he had fallen asleep, fully clothed, in his armchair. In a deep sleep, his heart had drifted to the only one who had ever captured it.

"Never mind the peas, Ida. I got good news for you. It's Lila. She's havin' a baby and guess who's gonna babysit?"

"Ach... I'm afraid to! Too many surprises from you, Nat. Now what?"

"Oh, Ida. Stop worryin'. I can do it."

"I know you can, Nat. And that's wonderful news about Lila. I'm so glad. But listen to me, Nat." Ida's tone took a serious turn.

Nat took note and looked at her intently.

"You've been a good father to the children," she continued. "You've been a good husband to me. Now, you must be a good friend."

"How so?" inquired Nat, perplexed.

"I'm not so sure myself, Nat. I wish I could tell you more. I should only be so smart. I truly don't know what tomorrow will bring. You can't predict in this life. Things seem to happen, maybe for a reason, maybe not. If there wasn't a bad snowstorm, you're safe and sound at home. Who knows? So, a snowstorm should come, but without Christmas lights on at Gus and Lenny's, maybe there wouldn't have been a pot of chicken soup or a garden. I don't know. You're lucky you met Stephen and Lila."

"You're a smart one, you are, Ida. But who's Lenny?"

"Never you should mind, Nat. The name's not important."

"Ida?"

"Yes, Nat?"

"I...I...feel pretty good. I think maybe I'm enjoyin' myself. You don't mind, do you?"

"Mind! Ach, I've been waiting four years. Enjoy all you want. I should only worry if you don't."

"Thank you, Ida."

"You shouldn't thank me, Nat. Just stick with the peas. And Nat, be a good friend."

"It's a done deal, Ida. But somehow I figure you knew that."

"I did," she whispered, the words fading into the dark.

❄❄

As the sun rose, Nat began to stir. Stretching his arms wide and arching his back, he opened his eyes and smiled to himself from deep within. Morning's sunlight streamed through the window blinds. He settled back into the chair, yawned and closed his eyes, letting himself be carried off to continued sleep.

Monday Morning

"HEY, POP!"

"Michael, my boy. How's the family?"

"Everyone is just fine, pop. How are you?"

"Things are hummin' along, Michael. Guess what?"

"You gave up chicken?"

Nat laughed into the telephone.

"Nope," he answered cheerfully. "Got the garden up and runnin'."

"You're kidding! It's been years."

"I know. Got some new friends, Stephen and Lila. Guess I didn't mention 'em to you before. Musta slipped my mind. Great kids, though. 'Bout your age. Helped me plant."

"You're making friends, pop?"

"Sure am!"

"Listen, pop. Are you feeling alright?"

"Never felt better. Why d'ya ask?"

There was a momentary silence on the phone as Michael paused.

"I don't know. You...you just sound different."

"How so?" asked Nat.

"I'm not sure," answered Michael. "You almost sound... happy."

"Nothin' wrong with that, I guess," chuckled Nat.

"Nothing at all. It's good to hear."

"So listen, Michael. When am I gonna see you and that lovely family of yours?"

"Well, we're all thinking of coming east this summer. Me and my family. Robert and his. How's that sound to you?"

"Wonderful! Made my day! And you can all meet my friends."

"We'll look forward to it."

"Send my love, Michael. I gotta run. Gotta water the garden."

"I will. I have to run too, pop. I'm on my way out the door to work. Tried calling you yesterday morning but you didn't answer."

"Musta been outside in the yard. Well, good-bye, son."

"Good-bye, pop."

❀❀

"Tell me, Lila, what is it?" whispered Maggie.

Maggie had walked across the hallway from her classroom to Lila's. It was just before 9:00 A.M. and the imminent arrival of the children. She had left her classroom doorway and approached Lila, who stood at the entrance to her own room. Ordinarily, if they hadn't had time to chit chat earlier in the morning, Maggie simply would have waved hello and the two would have caught up with one another during a break. But not today, not this Monday morning. Maggie did not wait. She saw something in Lila's face that she had seldom seen these past few years.

"Tell me, Lila." she repeated.

Lila smiled, enigmatically.

"Tell you what, Maggie?"

Maggie glanced to her left and right. No one appeared near enough to hear them.

"You look so contented this morning, Lila. Your face just has a…a glow about it. I know you well enough. I don't ask too many questions and I don't pry, but something is different, something is…"

"Shh…don't say anything, Maggie." Lila whispered, hardly able to contain herself.

Maggie waited, breathless.

"I'm pregnant," said Lila, beaming. "I've only told my parents and now you, Maggie."

They suddenly heard the clamor of the children.

"I'm so happy for you," smiled Maggie hurriedly, finding it difficult to mute her excitement. "How do you feel?"

"I feel great, just a little headache this morning." Lila lowered her voice. "Please don't let anyone else know", she said softly. "I just want to wait a while longer before I say anything."

"You've got my word, Lila. I'm just so thrilled for you."

Around the corner came the children, marching noisily along.

"Talk to you later," said Maggie, quickly giving Lila a kiss on the cheek. "Congratulations!"

"Thank you, Maggie."

Maggie turned and bounced back across the hallway, overjoyed for her friend.

Lila's students streamed through the doorway.

She wished them each a good morning. As good as mine, she thought to herself.

❦❦

"There aren't any guarantees. We can all see that now. I think this is as safe as you can get and you'll continue to have a steady income. I know it's an adjustment, Mr. Miles, but things will change again. We have to be positive." Stephen spoke reassuringly into the telephone.

"Thank you, Stephen. You know I'm a worry wart. The experts weren't so expert. You've always done right by me. I'll bet you're as conservative as I am," chuckled Mr. Miles.

"Maybe even more," answered Stephen, laughing. "Enjoy your Monday and try not to worry so much."

Stephen hung up the phone and mused out loud, "easier said than done."

He wasn't thinking of Mr. Miles, but of himself. As he leaned back in his chair and looked down at his desk, at the framed picture of Lila upon it, he thought of the myriad days of worry he had experienced while sitting right here. But not today. Even the papers and financial reports resting beside the computer monitor with its columns of numbers peering back at him, would not evoke worry today.

He got up from his desk and walked over to the window. He opened it on this Monday morning in late March, letting a plethora of numbers and worries fly out while fresh air and hopeful thoughts of himself and Lila wafted in. He stood there and breathed in deeply.

Nothin' But A Damn Shame

AFTER SEVENTY-FIVE YEARS, NAT KNEW all too well that bad news can arrive without even turning the page of a newspaper. The pea plants had not yet poked through the earth when he got the news. The phone rang as he sat in his armchair reading the daily paper, housebound on a rainy afternoon. He quickly walked to the kitchen, grabbed the receiver and put it to his ear.

After listening intently, he simply closed his eyes and nodded his head from side to side, stammering into the phone, "I'm...I'm sorry, Stephen. Just tell me what I can do."

"I don't know," responded Stephen. "I just don't know."

Stephen provided some details but did not linger for long on the telephone.

Nat had but one thought in mind, despite the rain. He hurriedly threw on a coat and grabbed an umbrella, then unhesitatingly headed out the front door. He almost tripped down the porch steps in his haste.

"Poor kids," he mumbled to himself. "Sometimes it just don't end."

He walked against a cold rain and strong wind. He tilted his umbrella forward, trying to repel the wind. It was to no avail. It seemed an eternity, a walk that would ordinarily take only fifteen minutes. He knew. He had made that walk so often. Finally, he stood at the hospital entrance, trembling.

"Soaked through," he grumbled, looking down at his feet while shaking out the umbrella.

He closed it and stepped closer to the automatic doors. They opened. He stopped, as if frozen to the spot. He continued to tremble.

"Been four long years since I stepped through those doors," he whispered, shaking his head.

People walked past him, on either side, through the doors he had opened.

He drew a long, deep breath of air and looked up towards the heavens. He stood up straight and braced himself, staring directly ahead.

"Gotta do it for the little lady," he said firmly.

He marched through the open doors.

"How can I help you?" asked the elderly man sitting behind the desk.

Nat had walked across the hospital lobby, remaining focused on the kindly looking gentleman behind the information desk. Fearful that he would change his mind, he had marshalled all of his concentration for that short walk.

"I would like to visit Lila Brook."

"Give me just a moment... here we are. She's in the ICU. Sign right there then go through the..."

"Believe me, I know how to get there," interrupted Nat with a sigh, as he was signing the register. He put down the pen and looked directly at the elderly gentleman.

The man hesitated for a moment and then said, "I understand." They both nodded.

✵✵

Nat quietly traversed those all too familiar hallways, seeing some visitors standing alone waiting beside doorways or others together, talking in the brightly lit corridors. He glanced into open doorways, spying some patients alone and others with company. He saw an array of smiling faces and sad ones. A picture of him and his boys huddled together outside Ida's door talking to one another came to mind. He just continued to walk, approaching the ICU, trying so hard not to think the unthinkable.

He turned a corner and pushed open a set of double doors. They swung closed behind him and he slowly walked along a very narrow corridor, a nurse's station to his left and rooms lining the right. He quickly surveyed those rooms as he passed them, looking for Stephen in each one. Finally, he arrived at his destination, peering into the last room and seeing Stephen sitting in a chair at the bedside of an immobile figure shrouded in white linens, surrounded by an assemblage of machinery. Stephen's face looked ashen, his body gaunt. Nat was speechless. His heart was in his throat.

"Nat?" Stephen rose from the chair and approached the door. Nat extended his hand.

"You didn't have to come," whispered Stephen, taking Nat's hand.

"Yes, I did." Nat entered the room.

"Here, sit down," said Stephen. "Look at you," he continued, "you're sopping wet. You didn't walk here, did you?"

"It don't matter," shrugged Nat. "Just wanted to be here."

He sat in the lone chair in the room, at the head of the bed and looked at Lila. Amidst all of the tubes and wires that enveloped her, he saw the warm-hearted, beautiful face he had come to know. Stephen stood beside him. There was silence but for the intermittent beeps of the machines as they continually registered all the different numbers that monitored the progression of a life.

"She just collapsed, Nat. Right in my arms. Right in the kitchen."

Nat looked up at Stephen, at the pain that permeated his face. He thought about the baby. He did not ask. He feared the answer.

"You don't gotta say another word, Stephen. We can just stay quiet."

"It's alright, Nat." Stephen inhaled deeply and continued.

"She said she had an awful headache. She barely finished telling me and she fell. I...I don't understand, Nat. They said it was an aneurysm. They said that it can just happen and they don't know why. What, what does that mean? They stopped the hemorrhaging. But...they, they don't know if she'll recover. It could hemorrhage again. I just don't understand. Hadn't she had enough pain already? She...she doesn't deserve this."

Nat looked again at Lila's face. Her beauty was not diminished by the uncharacteristic paleness of her skin or her now sallow cheeks. He closed his eyes and out of the blue the story of Sleeping Beauty popped into his head. He remembered Ida reading it to the boys. He wished it could only be that simple, that Stephen would gallantly bend toward her lips, kiss them, and Lila would open her eyes. The thought quickly vanished and he opened his eyes. Hers were still closed.

"Too many things beyond understandin' in this world," he offered. "You just gotta keep your chin up, Stephen. You been eatin'? You gotta keep your strength up, too."

"Not much, Nat."

"You must, pal."

"Yeah, I guess," Stephen shrugged.

"Listen, I'll sit a little while longer then I oughta go."

"Whenever you'd like, Nat. I appreciate your coming."

"You gotta get some rest too, Stephen."

"I'll try."

"You need anything, you just ask."

"Thanks, Nat."

The automatic doors slowly shut behind him as Nat left the hospital. The rain had let up a bit. With the umbrella tucked under his arm, he pounded his right fist into the open palm of his left hand.

"Nothin' but a damn shame," he grumbled.

He walked home.

Early Mourning

$\mathcal{A}$S THE MONITORS SURROUNDING LILA went awry before his eyes, Stephen recalled her words from what seemed a long ago morning in the tent. "What if something happens to one of us?" she had asked.

Her fear came to fruition. Something did...to her. A swarm of white clad people rushed into the room as Stephen stood by in horror. A second hemorrhage took her and...

As acquainted as he was with the arrival of bad news, a consequence of his longevity, Nat certainly knew as well that things often went from bad to worse. This knowledge did not inoculate him from the three simple words that he clearly heard Stephen say over the phone.

"She's gone, Nat."

Within the total arc of his life to that moment, Nat Zeigler had known Lila Brook but a very short time. Time was not an accurate measure of his feelings. With three simple words his heart broke.

Once again, Nat had not fared well in inclement weather. The walk to the hospital in that relentless downpour left him with an awful cold. He had received the phone call from Stephen while lying in bed, his night table littered with tissues, half empty glasses of water, and a thermometer which he did not even know how to use. He had dragged himself out of bed to answer the phone and dragged himself back afterwards, even more depleted.

He was laid up for days. He thought of many things, among them a bowl of chicken soup. There was none to be had. He had eaten the last of Lila's soup while recovering from that earlier cold.

He missed Lila's wake and her funeral. Even if he had had the energy to go, he wouldn't have wanted to get anyone sick, especially Stephen. Resigned to waiting it out, hoping to regain his strength as quickly as possible, he rested. Finally, after a few days, he felt well enough to leave the house. Early in the morning he set out, with but one destination.

Turning the corner onto Sycamore, Nat spied three people gathered on Stephen's front steps. One was Stephen. The other two, a man and woman, he did not recognize. He stopped short and waited a moment as he saw them each embrace Stephen. As they descended the steps, he could see that they were an older couple, closer in age to himself.

He watched as they walked toward a waiting car. They turned toward Stephen, waved good-bye, and entered the car. It pulled away from the curb and as it passed by, Nat quickly read the words displayed on the passenger side doors, "Airport Limousine." He continued walking.

Stephen saw him approach and started down the steps.

They stood inches apart.

Nat sneezed.

"Excuse me, pal," he said.

They hugged.

"I'm so sorry, buddy." Nat stared at Stephen. He was startled by the familiar face before him. Only it wasn't Stephen's, it was his, the face in his own mirror, staring back at him after Ida died. It was the face of indescribable sorrow, a countenance of grief beyond words.

"I know you are, Nat."

"I'm sorry I missed..."

"Don't be, Nat. I understand. She would have too. She even would have taken care of you if she were..." Stephen's voice trailed off into silence.

"I know she woulda. Musta been a big crowd. I'm sure anyone who met her fell in love with the little lady."

"Thanks, Nat. Please come inside."

Nat followed Stephen up the steps and into the house.

Once inside, Stephen collapsed onto the couch.

"I'm exhausted, Nat. I don't know what to do first. I miss her so much."

With his elbows perched on his knees and his head resting in the palms of his hands, Stephen sobbed.

Nat sat beside him and put his arm around Stephen's shoulder.

"It's alright, pal," he whispered. "I'm right here."

Stephen didn't respond.

Nat didn't say a word. He looked around the room as Stephen sat silently beside him. The living room looked as neat and tidy as the last time he had been there.

Nat cleared his throat.

"A cup of tea," he finally said. "Let me make you a nice hot cup of tea."

"What's that, Nat?" asked Stephen. "What's that you said?"

"A cup of tea," Nat repeated. "Let me make you a cup of tea."

"Thank you, Nat," murmured Stephen.

"Sure thing. You just sit tight and I'll be right back."

Once inside the kitchen, Nat slumped into a chair at the table. He gazed around the empty kitchen, at the clear countertop, the bare table at which he sat. His mind reeled with images of Lila and Stephen and himself and pots and vegetables and chicken parts and water boiling and steam rising and soup cooking and smiling faces...

And there was only really himself and silence.

"Poor kid," he mumbled aloud, filling in the void of his own silence. "Damn crazy world. Seen my friends go. One by one. And Ida too. Old. All of us old. But a young kid like that. Makes no sense. No sense at all." He rubbed his eyes with the back of his hand.

"Tea, tea," he continued aloud. "Put up some water for Stephen. That's what I came in here for. Tea for Stephen."

He rose from the chair and glanced at the stove, spotting the teapot.

Better make a cup for myself, he thought.

He filled the teapot, put a light under it, got two cups from a cabinet, and located the teabags in a canister on the counter.

"Be there in a minute," he shouted.

"I'm...I'm, it's alright, Nat. Whenever."

"Damn shame," Nat murmured under his breath.

He returned to the living room with the two cups of tea.

"Here you go," he said, extending his arm to Stephen.

Stephen looked up at him, vacantly, and took the cup.

Nat recognized that gaze. He had seen it too in his own reflection. It was the face of a person looking not ahead, but inward to the past.

He sat beside Stephen.

"Drink your tea," he implored.

Stephen sipped.

"Kitchen's clean as a whistle," said Nat, trying to elicit something, anything from Stephen. "Living room, too."

"Lila's mother," answered Stephen absentmindedly. "She did a lot of cleaning. They just left for the airport."

"Ah," responded Nat.

"How's the garden?" asked Stephen. "It meant a lot to her. Helping you get your garden started again."

"I know," answered Nat, fighting back tears. "It's comin' along."

"When my parents..." Stephen gripped the teacup with both hands. "But...but this is different. I...I can't describe it. I feel numb. I'm so tired, Nat."

"You gotta get some sleep, Stephen. You need to rest. How 'bout you finish your tea and get a little shut eye?"

Stephen was compliant. "Alright," he answered listlessly.

He drank down the last of his tea.

Nat took the cup from him, walked into the kitchen and put both cups in the sink.

Upon his return, he took Stephen by the arm and walked with him to the bedroom.

"Now just get undressed and get under those covers. That's an order, pal! A good night's sleep'll do you a world of good. I'll let myself out in a little while. Don't worry, I'll lock the door behind me." He clicked on a lamp.

Stephen got into bed and rolled onto his side.

Nat noticed a chair in the corner of the room and pulled it beside the bed.

"I'll just sit a while," he said.

Nat could hear muffled sobs. He waited patiently until he could see the blanket rising and falling rhythmically and that all was quiet. He rose from his chair and walked around to the other side of the bed. Stephen was asleep, tears having run down his cheek, leaving the pillow damp near the corner of his mouth. Nat turned off the lamp and tiptoed out of the room, leaving the door slightly ajar. He walked to the kitchen.

Nat stood over the kitchen sink, rinsing out the teacups as he stared out of the window into a night illuminated by a full moon. He wished Ida was there to talk with. He wished he could soothe Stephen's pain. He wished that he had a recipe whose ingredients would conjure up only memories that could efface one's sorrow. He would start cooking at the drop of a hat. He wished...

He dried the teacups and placed them on the countertop beside the sink. He carefully folded the dish towel and set it beside the cups. He left the kitchen, took a look in on Stephen, and let himself out of the house.

Sweet And Sour

ONCE INSIDE HIS OWN HOUSE, Nat headed straight for his bed-room. Exhausted, he immediately undressed, tossed his clothes across a chair, and literally fell into bed. Though he wait-ed, sleep did not arrive. He tossed and turned and finally gave in to an unwanted wakefulness. He wished the day to end. It simply would not. He sat up in bed and stared into the darkness.

Maybe could use a little somethin' stronger than tea this time round, he thought to himself. He reached towards the lamp, turned it on and got out of bed. In bathrobe and slippers he walked to the kitchen.

"Hmm…a nice glass of wine," he said aloud. "Kill two birds with one stone. Knock me out and help the circulation. Or so I hear."

He turned on the kitchen light, squinted, and opened the cabinet that held his small supply of liquor. He parted the bot-tles and labored to read the labels without his glasses, until he figured he had a bottle of red wine in hand. He pulled it out over some other bottles.

"Ah, a merlot. Could be older than me," he mused aloud.

After grabbing a glass from the dish drainer, he realized he needed a corkscrew. He couldn't even remember where one might be. It had been so long since he had need of one. He rummaged through the countertop drawers to no avail. He began to search the overhead cabinets, peering behind bowls and cups, cans and boxes.

While on tiptoes, he spied something which he thought resembled a corkscrew nestled in the rear of a cluttered shelf. He extended his arm and groped for the object. His hand landed on the corners of what felt like a small metal box. He grabbed hold of it and pulled it out. Perplexed, he put it on the counter and reached back in to retrieve the corkscrew. He quickly had it in hand.

"Heck of a lot a work for a glass of wine," he mumbled.

He put the box on the kitchen table, opened the wine, and poured himself a glass.

Settling into a chair at the table, he took a sip of wine and stared at the box.

He wondered.

"Hmm...looks like a file box of some sort," he said, scratching his head.

He wondered some more.

"Hmm...maybe my Ida had a coupla dancin' partners she didn't tell me about. Well, here goes nothin'."

He opened the lid to see a plethora of papers crammed together. He pulled a few out. A quick glance, even without his glasses, and he knew.

"Holy...she was right!" he exclaimed.

He emptied the glass of wine in a single gulp and poured another.

"Recipes! That Ida of mine!"

He scattered the contents of the box across the table. After retrieving his reading glasses from the living room, he browsed amongst the papers. There were small scraps and large ones, folded sheets of paper, and some that appeared brittle and brown with age. A few were barely legible. Others were stained with what Nat surmised were cooking ingredients. He did not recognize all of the handwriting. Some was Ida's. Some might have been her mother's.

Noodle...

Glazed...

Chocolate...

He drank down the second glass of wine and poured another.

He randomly picked up one of the folded sheets of paper and opened it.

SWEET AND SO...

He stopped.

"The meatballs!" he shouted.

He could barely contain himself. He drank his third glass of wine and poured yet another.

He stared at the paper. Words were intermingled with reddish purple blotches.

"Gotta slow down on the wine," he advised himself.

He ran his finger across the paper. The blotches did not disappear.

"So, Ida wasn't so neat," he shrugged.

He took a sip of wine. Why had he never seen Ida with any of these recipes in hand? Some of them looked so old and worn. When was the last time that she had actually pulled one out of the box? He knew that all of her recipes were in her head. She could have cooked anything half asleep.

He stopped wondering and emptied his glass.

"Ida," he said aloud, in the steadiest voice he could summon, "if you don't mind I'm gonna try and cook up some of your meatballs for my friend, Stephen. I can't read all the ingre... ingredients too clearly but I'm gonna give it a shot. I gotta help my friend and he's gotta eat. I'm gonna start cookin' as soon as, as soon as..."

Nat folded his arms across the table and rested his head in the bend of his elbow. He closed his eyes.

"Tomorrow," he yawned. "First thing in the ..."

He fell asleep, amidst for him, what would have amounted to culinary heaven.

With A Pinch Of Friendship

NAT AWOKE WITH A POUNDING headache. He looked at the kitchen clock.

"Six in the morning," he groused.

He rubbed his temples with open palms.

"Geez, haven't felt like this in I don't know how long. Could be my drinkin' days are over. Probably got the best circulation in town this mornin'."

He looked out across the table at all of the recipes.

"Supermarket opens in an hour. Got some work ahead of me."

He lumbered to the bathroom and showered and shaved.

After getting dressed, he stopped in the kitchen and grabbed the recipe for the meatballs, stuffing it into his pocket. He hurried out the front door.

Nat walked at a brisk pace, reaching the market in no time at all. He pulled out a shopping cart from the row in front of the store windows and hurried inside. He put on his reading glasses and retrieved the recipe from his pocket. Scanning the sheet, he tried awfully hard to fill in the letters that had been effaced with time. Nat was familiar with where to find the staples that provided him his daily needs. He wasn't so sure about some of the things on the list.

"Jelly?" he scratched his head. "What is that? A condiment?"

There were very few shoppers at that hour and Nat was able to navigate the aisles easily. With a little assistance along the way, he was able to locate everything on the list that he knew was not in the pantry at home. After comparing the contents of his cart with the list and concluding that he had everything, he got on the checkout line.

Once home, he spread all of the ingredients out on the table and got one of Ida's pots from a cabinet. With rolled up sleeves and little clue as to what he was doing, he began following the recipe's directions. A short while later and the entire kitchen was a mess. Measuring cups, bottles, cans, jars, spices, bowls, spoons, ladles...all lay strewn about the kitchen.

"From such a small piece of paper, how could there be such a big mess?" he wondered aloud.

He lifted the lid on the simmering pot of meatballs and inhaled

"Stephen's gonna like these," he smiled through the sweetly scented cloud of air that surrounded his head.

The meatballs simmered throughout the day.

Nat cleaned the kitchen and decided upon a nap.

He awakened around dusk and hurried to the kitchen to check on the meatballs. He tasted one, smacked his lips together and nodded with approval.

"Just like on the holiday!" he exclaimed.

He spooned out the meatballs, one by one, onto a large tray, and put it aside to cool off. After washing and drying the pot, he covered the tray with tin foil and readied himself to leave.

Nat Zeigler walked down Sycamore Street once again, this time carrying a simple offering, made with the sweet promise of friendship in order to assuage the sour taste of misfortune.

The School Bag

NAT KNOCKED ON STEPHEN'S DOOR with his right hand, balancing the tray in his left. He knocked several times and waited. Finally, Stephen appeared, looking worn and red-eyed.

"Gettin' worried there for a minute," said Nat uneasily. "Been here a while."

"Oh, I'm sorry, Nat. I was just sitting and thinking. I guess I got lost in my own little world. Didn't hear a thing."

"Don't pay it any mind, pal," responded Nat, relieved. "Just grab this." He thrust the tray of meatballs towards Stephen.

"What's this?" asked Stephen, looking puzzled as he took the tray with both hands.

"Meatballs. Sweet and sour. Ida's best. Made 'em myself from scratch."

"But where did you get…how did you…?"

"Never mind that," Nat broke in, "we're gonna just enjoy 'em. Put a little meat on your bones."

"I don't know, Nat. I mean, don't get me wrong. I appreciate what you've done but I really haven't had much of an appetite. I haven't eaten and I…"

"You're gettin' thin as a rail," interrupted Nat. "I got recipes you wouldn't believe. We're gonna get you back to fightin' weight in no time."

Stephen evinced a half-hearted smile.

"Sure, Nat." It was all he could muster.

Nat followed Stephen to the kitchen and couldn't help but notice the clutter on the kitchen table.

Stephen put the tray on the counter and turned to Nat.

"I'll clear the table, Nat. I've just been sorting through some things. You know your way around the kitchen. Would you mind getting out two plates and some silverware?"

"Be my pleasure."

As Nat was reaching for two plates, he heard behind his back a dull thud and the tinny sound made by metal objects crashing against one another. He quickly turned.

"You o.k.?" he asked.

Stephen was kneeling on the floor beside a leather shoulder bag, its contents spread about on the floor. His eyes began to water.

"Here, let me help you," offered Nat. He knelt beside Stephen.

"It's Lila's school bag," said Stephen. "I was going to go through it tonight."

"What d'ya call this?" asked Nat. He had picked something up. "Looks like the letter V upside down."

"That's a compass, Nat. You use it in math."

"Been so long. Sure the boys musta used one. Just can't remember. Ida helped 'em with their homework."

As Nat was finishing his sentence, Stephen spotted a pen lying amidst an assortment of colored pencils. He picked it up and simply held it in his hand, staring at it.

"Sharp lookin' pen," said Nat.

"I bought it for Lila when she started teaching. Seems like yesterday," sighed Stephen. "I didn't even know she still had it. Look, Nat."

Stephen rolled the pen between his thumb and index fingers, turning it ever so slightly so that the letters LB appeared before Nat's eyes.

Nat looked admiringly at the gold lettering engraved in the shiny black finish of the pen.

"Got the little lady's initials. Beautiful, pal. Bet she used it everyday."

Stephen breathed in deeply and exhaled, deflated.

"How about those meatballs," he suggested, changing the subject.

"Anything you say, buddy."

Together, they retrieved everything that had fallen out of Lila's school bag and began putting it all back.

"Didn't use one of these in my day," said Nat, holding a calculator in his hand.

"Why don't you keep it, Nat," suggested Stephen.

"I couldn't. Don't even know how to use one. Besides, numbers are up your alley. Not my cup of tea."

"I'm not so sure of that anymore, Nat. I'm not so sure of a lot of things anymore. It seems like the whole world just turned upside down in the blink of an eye. Everything I thought I knew... maybe I don't. Maybe two and two don't always equal four. I never thought I would ever be without..." Stephen swallowed hard, choking back tears. "Lila," he finished the sentence.

"No, nothin' is written in stone," responded Nat, shaking his head. "Easy thing to forget in this busy world."

"Keep it, Nat. Keep the calculator."

"If you insist," shrugged Nat. "But anytime you want it back, you just ask."

Stephen put Lila's school bag away. He put the meatballs in the oven to warm up and then finished clearing the table. Nat set it.

They sat across from one another, the tray of meatballs between them.

Nat dished them out.

"She would have been a wonderful mother," whispered Stephen, hunched over his plate as if the weight of the world was upon his shoulders.

"No doubt about it," murmured Nat, his heart in his throat.

Stephen lifted his gaze and looked directly at Nat, perhaps truly seeing him for the first time that evening.

"I'm sorry, Nat," he apologized. "I haven't even asked about you since you got here. I just go on about my own misery. It's unfair of me to throw this all out at you. I'm sorry."

"Listen, Stephen. You say whatever's on your mind. I wanna hear whatever you got to say. Just do me one favor. Eat a meatball. At least one."

Stephen's lips formed the hint of a smile. He picked up his fork.

"Ida's best!" exclaimed Nat.

Lila's Gift

STEPHEN BROOK SAT ALONE IN his house. Surrounding him were all of the familiar things he and Lila had acquired together over the years, the things that reflect a marriage of tastes, the things that adorn a home. They brought him little comfort. They only reminded him of her and their life together that had prematurely ended. It pained him to think of what might have been.

He thought that he would find comfort in working, or if not comfort, then at least a diversion from the relentless onslaught of memory. He found neither comfort nor diversion while sitting behind his desk at work. Very little added up anymore, least of all the numbers that crossed his desk, day in and day out. At the bank, his mind had become a repository of all things that Lila's name was apt to conjure: regrets for words spoken and unspoken, the longing to relive moments that in retrospect all seemed idyllic, the remembrance of silly, meaningless incidents, but most of all the simple image of her. He sat listlessly at his desk. Day after day. Adrift in the present while looking over his shoulder toward the past, he had no vision of the future. For a man of so practical a nature, he hadn't the inkling of a plan. Not anyone or anything could seemingly rescue him from the conflagration of memories that threatened to engulf him.

※※

As the season changed from spring to summer, Stephen remained the same.

Nat had grown terribly worried. He became increasingly fearful that without Lila, Stephen would simply fade away, becoming a virtual recluse despite his job and daily routine. Nat thought about this a lot. He had known someone just like that. Knew 'im like a book, he thought to himself. Can't let that happen. Kid's way too young, way too young for that.

So Nat came by often, keeping Stephen company and bringing him home cooked meals, ones that he had cooked. For in the span of three short months Nat Zeigler had become the master chef of Birch Road. His repertoire included pot roast, meatballs, noodle pudding, rice pudding, chocolate layer cake, and turkey with stuffing. The menu was ever expanding and Stephen was the recipient of Nat's growing culinary skills. Ida might have been looking on, aghast at the state of her kitchen, yet smiling deep within.

On a warm summer's evening in mid July, Nat telephoned Stephen and invited him over for dinner. It was his first stab at stuffed cabbage.

"Been cookin' up a storm, pal," Nat said excitedly. "Knocked myself out. How 'bout comin' by here for dinner. Save me the walk over."

"Sure, Nat," replied Stephen, with little conviction in his voice. "I guess it wouldn't hurt for me to get out a bit."

"Good. Come through the back. You know, through the gate."

❄❄

Stephen pushed open the gate and immediately realized how easily it opened into the yard. He looked down to see that the overgrown grass had disappeared, a short well groomed lawn in its stead. Barely looking up, he walked toward the wrought iron table and chairs, where he and Lila had once sat. In his path was the old push lawnmower, only it didn't look so old to him anymore.

"Oiled it up and gave it a good once over!" exclaimed Nat, coming out of the back door. "Good to see you, buddy," he greeted Stephen.

"You did a nice job on the lawn. What do you charge?" asked Stephen, his voice flat and his face without expression, despite his attempt at a little joke.

"Not a cent for you. Just gotta ask. But never mind that. Grab a seat."

Stephen joined Nat at the table. The two widowers sat across from one another. Upon the table were a single tomato and beside it a narrow, white box about six inches long and an inch wide. Stephen noticed both of these but did not think anything out of the ordinary. Nat knew otherwise.

"Listen, Stephen," said Nat in an inviting yet unmistakably emphatic tone.

The earnestness in Nat's voice registered in Stephen's mind. He suddenly snapped out of his desultory funk and stared intently at Nat.

"Listen," repeated Nat. "I'm no rocket scientist, Stephen, but I've been doin' a lot of thinkin'. Remember when you first met me? I was all bundled up in my coat and my hat. Could barely stand up in that blizzard. I was nothin' but an old man. Now look at me! Got a lot of spunk. But more important, pal, look over there."

Nat pointed across the yard.

Stephen looked beyond Nat's outstretched arm. He saw for the first time what he might have seen, while crossing the yard, if he had only lifted his eyes to see anything beyond his own thoughts.

"Oh, my!" he exclaimed, clapping his hands together.

A broad smile crossed Nat's face.

Stephen marveled at the rows of plump red tomatoes that dangled from vines which had wound around wooden stakes, one stake after another after another.

Nat turned back to Stephen.

"Look at that, Stephen. Who woulda ever thought? The thing is pal...life don't stop. It just don't stop."

Nat hesitated for an instant and breathed in deeply.

"Stephen, she was a better teacher than anyone could ever know. Mark my words."

"Thank you, Nat," said Stephen, faintly.

"Now," continued Nat, "that tomato next to the little box is for you. A promise is a promise. That's the first one to come off a vine. It's yours. If you'd like, we can throw it in the salad later. Up to you."

"You're a good man, Nat." Stephen took the tomato. He nodded and pursed his lips with approval as he held it in his hand.

"Well, hold on a minute, pal. I'm still goin'. Like I said, I'm no rocket scientist but I came up with an idea I wanna run past you. Give a listen."

Stephen just sat quietly. He couldn't imagine what might be coming next.

"I know you're not so happy at work. You told me the numbers just aren't addin' up there. You're not so happy anywhere. Believe me, I understand. Well, the memory's got a little life left in her yet. I remember how the little lady said you two met. Summer camp. Workin' with kids. And I remember you sayin' at breakfast that lovely mornin' we made the soup that if you were a teacher you woulda taught math. So I decided to put two and two together, do a little math myself. Open the box. It's a little something for you."

Stephen sat dumbfounded. He didn't know what to say. He reached for the box.

Nat watched closely as Stephen took the box in his hand.

Stephen stared at it, puzzled.

"Go ahead, buddy," coaxed Nat.

Stephen lifted the cover and put it aside. With his thumb and index fingers, he peeled away a thin layer of crumpled tissue paper. He stared into the box and then up at Nat.

"Not gonna hire me so fast in the gift wrap department at Macy's, that's for sure," mused Nat, suddenly embarrassed.

Stephen reached into the box and took out a thin pen with a shiny black finish. Engraved along its side, in gold lettering, were the initials SB.

"Like I said, just an idea, pal. Somethin' to think about. I mean you teachin'. Kids, maybe them numbers'll add up right again ...what better way to..."

Nat paused as a little more than the hint of a smile appeared on Stephen's face.

"First time I seen anything approachin' a smile on you since..."

"Thank you, Nat. I'm just flabbergasted." Stephen's voice rose with emotion. He wiped away a tear. "Do you think I could do it? I mean I'm no kid anymore, myself."

"Look at the garden. There's your answer."

"Who says you're not a rocket scientist," whispered Stephen.

"Come on, pal. Whatd'ya say we have some dinner?"

"What did you make this time?"

"Stuffed cabbage."

"I'm game."

They stood up. Stephen grabbed the tomato. He took the pen, slowly ran his finger over the engraved letters and then placed it in his shirt pocket. As they walked across the patio to the house, Nat threw his arm around Stephen's shoulder.

"Everything is gonna be fine," he said.

"Thanks, Nat."

"By the way, do you like Merlot?"

Stephen Alone

"HEY, PAL. HOW YA FIXED for onions? Thinkin' a makin' potato pancakes tonight."

"Hang on a second, Nat. I'll check." Stephen cocked his head to the side, balancing the phone in the crook of his neck as he opened the refrigerator to peruse its contents. There was little to survey. He closed the door. "Sorry, Nat. No onions. Not much of anything to tell the truth," he sighed.

"Guess I'll have to go to the supermarket. Can't make Ida's pancakes without 'em. Must be something I can get for you."

"I could use some milk. Would you mind? Two percent."

"I know you're studyin' to be a math teacher, pal. Got all them numbers in your head, but milk is milk. One percent, two percent...it's a hundred percent milk no matter how you slice it."

"Thanks, Nat," Stephen laughed.

"Wanna come along with me? Get out for a little fresh air?"

"Maybe another time," yawned Stephen. "I'm really tired and I still have alot of reading to do tonight."

"I'll stop by on my way home and drop off the milk. Won't take me long."

"That sounds fine. Just keep ringing the bell until I get there just in case I've fallen asleep. I've been doing that a lot lately. Just sitting up, right in my chair. Never did that before."

"Know the feelin', pal. See ya in a while."

"Be careful, Nat."

Stephen hung up the phone and turned his attention to the thick textbook sitting on the kitchen table. He picked it up and carried it into the living room, settling into the armchair adjacent to the front window and letting the book rest on his lap. He looked down at it in disbelief. Had the summer truly come and gone already? Had he actually signed on for the fall semester in a night class at the local college, taking a course in education? Was he once again beginning to derive pleasure from his job, giving his clients his undivided attention? Was it all a dream? Closing his eyes, he answered yes to the first three questions and no to the fourth. He assured himself that he wasn't dreaming it all. In fact, he knew all too well what a long, slow haul it would be, going to school part-time at night.

Just then a late autumn breeze wafted in through the open window, caressing his face. He thought of her. The breeze carried with it the scent of her hair, or so he imagined. He breathed in deeply, and suddenly, to his surprise, juxtaposed the sweet smell of Lila's hair with Nat's quest for onions. Funny, the things that trigger a memory, he thought to himself. For now in his mind's eye he could clearly see Lila standing over the stove, stirring the chicken soup as he approached her. He had put his arms around her waist and could now recall the pungent smell of onions that had mingled in her hair. He smiled to himself and opened his eyes to find himself inescapably alone. The acknowledgement of being alone, a fact which faced him daily, was still alien to his heart. Though independent of mind, he and Lila had been inseparable all these many years. He looked down at the book on his lap in the waning light of an autumn evening.

"Educational Psychology", he said aloud, staring at the book's cover. "I guess you're never too old to learn something new." He paused a moment. "Or is it too young?" he quipped into the cool breeze, his voice cutting the air with an unintentional edge of bitterness. He quickly caught himself and stopped. "No self-pity," he admonished himself. After taking a deep breath, he opened the book to the assigned chapter, "Increasing Students' Self-Esteem". After reading a paragraph, he suddenly was accosted by another memory. A quick snapshot of himself, Lila, and Nat, in the restaurant, flashed to mind. He could clearly see Lila's glowing face, imbued with delight, as she told him about little Emily's mastery of her letters. Swiftly did that memory dissipate. In its stead, Stephen was suddenly filled with a sense of apprehension. Talk about self-esteem, could he ever match Lila's ability to make kids feel good about themselves? He wondered aloud. "She just had a way of connecting with children. She made them feel important. She was a natural. And me, what can I..." He shrugged his shoulders and reached into his shirt pocket to retrieve his pen, wishing to underline the last sentence of the paragraph. Looking at the pen and his initials engraved on its side brought a smile to his face. He hesitated for an instant and then to an empty room said, "I can do this. I'm good with people. I know it's not just about numbers. And I'm not a quitter!" He stared at the pen in his hand. "I'll pick up right where

Lila left off!" he exclaimed. He turned the page and continued reading, his pen at the ready.

❀❀

Nat pulled out a shopping cart from the long row of carts and swung it around with the alacrity that marked his little shopping expeditions. Through the sliding doors he went, past the display of assorted flower bouquets, around the mountain of end of season cantaloupes, and straight towards the onions. He grabbed a three pound bag and headed to the opposite side of the supermarket for the milk. Scampering along, seemingly with all the time in the world, he suddenly stopped short.

"Apple sauce!" he heard himself exclaim. "Can't eat potato pancakes without applesauce. Just can't get away from them condiments!" Knowing that he had just passed that aisle, he whipped the cart around and made a quick left turn.

Crash! Rose Pierce's hand held basket flew from her grasp and went skittering down the condiment aisle as Nat's cart hit it. Fortunately, it didn't hit Rose.

"Oh, my!" gasped Rose, watching in dismay as her few groceries tumbled out of the basket and went sliding along the floor.

Nat darted from behind the cart, shot past Rose, quickly stammering, "so sorry, ma'am", as he ran down the aisle, frantically tracking down all of her groceries. Luckily, there was nothing breakable, and one by one, Nat retrieved everything.

Rose had already picked up her basket and stood patiently, having quickly gotten over her initial shock. She watched, undeniably bemused, as Nat approached her, cradling in his arms a tube of toothpaste, four bananas, a head of lettuce, and a small container of olive oil.

"Sorry again, ma'am," uttered Nat, a little out of breath and more than a bit befuddled by the unexpected excitement. He stood immobile, unable to put one thing back in the basket for fear he would ultimately drop everything.

"Here, let me help you," offered Rose, reaching for the toothpaste. "I wish I had your energy," she smiled from behind her gold framed glasses, accentuating the creases in her face. "You certainly did scoot down the aisle."

Nat remained flummoxed while Rose continued to refill her basket.

"There. No harm done," she nodded to Nat, her groceries all returned. "Right back where we started from."

Nat finally found his voice, put at ease by Rose's matter of fact manner.

"Maybe there oughta be a law 'bout drivin' a shoppin' cart after a certain age," he suggested with the beginning of a smile.

"I'm thinking of giving it up myself," responded Rose, gesturing towards her basket.

"You sure you're alright?" asked Nat, his smile quickly evolving into a measure of concern.

"I'm perfectly fine. And you? That's the most excitement I've ever had in a supermarket."

"None the worse for wear," answered Nat. "Don't even remember what I came down this aisle for. By the way though, I'm forgettin' my manners." Nat offered his hand to Rose. "Nat Zeigler. Pleased to meet you."

Rose extended hers.

They shook.

"Rose Pierce," she said, "and I believe I heard someone shout 'applesauce' just before you came around the corner. Could that have been you?"

"That was me," grinned Nat.

"It's right over there." Rose pointed across the aisle.

Nat glanced quickly in that direction and then turned to Rose.

"Well, nice to meet you, Rose Pierce."

"Likewise, Nat Zeigler."

"I guess I should finish up," continued Nat, hesitating for an instant.

"So should I," responded Rose.

Nat grabbed the front of his shopping cart and pulled it forward past Rose. He took a few steps towards the applesauce jars, glanced to his right, and reached for a jar. Rose had already turned the corner and disappeared from view.

"Nice lady," Nat mumbled. He put the jar in his cart and scratched his head. "Forgot what else I came in here for. Got onions, applesauce…milk, that's it! Milk for Stephen."

He continued down the aisle, turning left at the end and heading straight to the dairy section. As he crossed each aisle, he absent-mindedly peeked to his left, searchingly. Nothing he saw was out of the ordinary. He shrugged his shoulders. With his reading glasses on, he scanned the milk cartons. Locating what he thought Stephen might want, he took a half gallon and proceeded to the check-out counter.

Nat exited the supermarket and accompanied by the same autumn breeze that was now lulling Stephen to sleep, began a leisurely walk towards Stephen's house. With a tight grip on his lone shopping bag, he breathed in the fall air. Glancing up at the sky and the myriad stars that lit up the black landscape, he whispered to himself, "it's good to be alive old man, it's good to be alive."

✤✤

Stephen rubbed his eyes and looked down at the book which lay askance on his lap. He knew that he hadn't read very much before dozing off and wasn't quite sure how long he had slept before being awakened by the sound of the doorbell.

"I wonder who that could be?" he asked aloud, looking towards the door. Suddenly, he remembered. "Milk!"

"Wake up, pal!" Nat shouted from the other side of the door. "Shake a leg!"

"Sorry, Nat," said Stephen, opening the door, groggy eyed and yawning.

"Been ringin' the bell so long, think it cured my arthritis." Nat held up his forefinger. "Straight as an arrow. Was crooked ten minutes ago." He laughed.

"Sometimes, Nat, you're like a ray of sunshine," offered Stephen, grinning.

"Been called a lot of things, pal, but never a ray of sunshine," Nat responded with an even broader grin than Stephen's. "Used to be more like a dark cloud. But I don't have to tell you that." Nat stepped into the house. "Here." He reached into his shopping bag and pulled out the container of milk. "Just like the milkman when I was a kid. Used to deliver milk right to the front door. First thing in the mornin'. Only it was in bottles then."

"Thanks." Stephen took the container from Nat. "I'll be right back. Have a seat."

Nat dropped into a corner of the couch while Stephen went to put the milk in the refrigerator.

"Would you like a cup of coffee or tea?" Stephen called from the kitchen.

"Nothin', buddy. I'm just gonna sit a few minutes. You got homework to do and I got some cookin' ahead of me."

"Things must have been a lot different when you were a kid," said Stephen upon his return. "The world's changed so much since my childhood. I can't even imagine the changes you've seen."

"There's a lot I could tell ya, Stephen. A whole lot."

"I'm sure you could, Nat," answered Stephen, settling into the opposite corner of the couch. "I'll bet I could learn a…" Stephen wavered a moment, his sentence awaiting completion as his eyes welled up with tears. "Give me a second, Nat," he continued.

"Take all the time you need. I ain't goin' anywhere." Nat sat patiently and waited.

"I'm sorry, Nat," Stephen finally said, having collected himself. "That's the second time I've apologized in less than fifteen minutes," he tried to smile, his attempt at lightheartedness of little avail. He rubbed his eyes.

"What's on your mind, pal?" queried Nat in a soothing tone. "I'm all ears."

"That's just it, Nat. There's really nothing on my mind. I just seem to react to things. I never know to what or when. Ever since Lila died. Certain things set me off. Out of the clear blue."

"Nothin' strange about that. Bless the little lady." Nat closed his eyes, sighed deeply, and then opened them. "Takes time to pull yourself together," he said knowingly.

"I know," agreed Stephen, nodding his head. "I forgot how long it took when my parents passed away. Not two years apart from each other. Without Lila's support… I just thought of them. That's what popped into my head."

"They musta been young. And you too. Damn shame." Nat looked quizzically at Stephen. "What made ya think of 'em?" he asked.

"I guess there's a lot that they could have told me also, Nat. A lot I could have learned from them if there had been more time." Stephen paused and swallowed hard. "I miss them. And now Lila's gone. I feel so alone."

"Hold on a second there, buddy. Old Nat is right here and he ain't goin' anywhere any time soon. You can bet your house on it," exclaimed Nat, forcefully.

Stephen, momentarily taken aback by the energy impelling Nat's words, did not respond.

"Listen up, Stephen," Nat continued, not missing a beat. "I gotta tell ya. You're like a son to me. Yep. Like havin' a third son. And Lila. Coulda been the daughter me and Ida never had. Ida, she'd a loved 'er. So the short of it is, you're stuck with me. And after I tell ya about the milkman, I'm gonna tell ya about a buncha other things."

Nat stopped momentarily to catch his breath. "Don't gotta say a word. Just try and keep your spirits up."

"You know, Nat, there is something I want to say." As did unforeseen moments of melancholy and chance memories overcome him, so now did a sudden feeling of strong conviction envelop Stephen's heart.

"Go right ahead, pal," responded Nat.

"You remember that day at the rink, when we were sitting on the bench. You asked about Lila's parents and before I could completely answer, Lila was standing there with the hot chocolates."

"Sure do. Seemed like the conversation was upsettin' you a bit. Seemed like somethin' was up with Lila's folks. I let it go when you did."

"It was. But what I wanted to say is…" Stephen's characteristic sense of surety and clarity now came to his aid, as it had always been wont to do. "That as much as you may have looked upon Lila as a daughter, she may very well have sensed that you were closer to her ideal of a true father than she had ever gotten. She never said it in so many words but considering her relationship with her own father…"

"Not close, huh," Nat interjected. "Is that what you were gettin' to on the bench."

"Basically. Lila's parents were always distant, physically and emotionally. Especially her father. It pained her terribly."

"Can't understand that. Woulda been proud to be her father." Nat smiled broadly and shook his head approvingly.

"Thanks, Nat."

"And like I said, you're like a son to me. But, neither of my sons have seen what you have, Stephen. They lost their mother, my Ida, but the losses you've… Maybe I got the edge in years on ya, but not in what they call them matters of the heart. On that pal we can see eye to eye. I wish it wasn't so. Believe me."

"I wish so too, Nat," sighed Stephen. "I wish so, too."

"Listen, pal, no matter what, you keep pluggin' along. World needs all the big hearts it can get. Not enough of 'em to suit me. You care, buddy. I know you take good care a them clients a yours at the bank. You care about kids. You care about… about…me." Nat paused for a second, taking a deep breath.

"But ya gotta remember to take care a yourself, too," he said gently, his voice now barely above a whisper. "Gotta do it for her. I know it's what she'd want, pal."

"And I know that you're right," said Stephen, nodding in agreement. "I guess there's a lot that's only up to me now. She'd want me to..." Stephen paused, rubbing his forehead.

"Maybe smile a little now and then," said Nat, quickly finishing Stephen's sentence.

Stephen then did smile. "Yes, that too," he said.

"Good. Now enough of this talk. You go get some shut eye and when the potato pancakes are done, I'll give you a yell."

"I am exhausted," yawned Stephen.

"Talk ta you tomorrow then."

For a relatively short walk home that night, Nat Zeigler certainly had a long list of thoughts vying for attention in his mind. He thought about Stephen and their common misfortune. Despite his worry, he had confidence in Stephen, sensing in him a capacity to forge on. No, Nat had to admit to himself, Stephen wasn't like Michael and Robert. He wasn't a go getter like the two of them, didn't seem inclined to climb any ladders to success. But he had confidence that Stephen would make out alright with a good heart and positive outlook, even if it took a while to get there. Thinking about Michael and Robert, he wished they had been able to get east this past summer. They certainly had tried. Though disappointed, Nat understood. Things come up. Especially with kids. He thought about Lila, and if she had lived, he wondered, what a nice relationship they would have had. And, to his amazement, he thought of Rose Pierce, picturing her for a fleeting moment in his mind's eye and wondering why he hadn't mentioned his little mishap to Stephen.

He walked home, his path illuminated by a string of streetlights that helped to guide him.

Stephen locked the door and turned out the lights. Once inside his bedroom, he turned on the lamp on the night table beside Lila's side of the bed. He sat on the edge of the bed, gazing at Lila's pillow and reaching out to gently smooth the ripples in her pillow case. The supple silk, soft to his touch, reminded him of Lila's skin. He clicked off the lamp and stretched out on the bed, resting his head on her pillow. He felt neither lonely nor whole. He simply felt alone, without her, his other half. He lay there, in the darkness, waiting to fall asleep.

Bananas

PROFESSOR SKYLAR STEPPED AWAY FROM the lectern and cleared his throat. He glanced at his watch. "We'll take a ten minute break." He motioned to the clock on the wall. "Not a minute more. We still have much to cover."

Stephen closed his notebook and placed his pen beside it, yawning deeply after another restless night, a day's work, and an early evening class. His days were a welcome relief from his nights. Daytime activities, marked by routine and contact with others, if not their genuine company, distracted him from the burden of a singular thought. He truly knew, from the death of his parents, that his current feeling of pain and loss would recede from the forefront of his heart, in time. It would not disappear, but only recede, allowing to blossom a mosaic of thoughts and memories that would induce warmth and not suffering. Unfortunately, what he knew did not quite assuage what he presently felt.

Despite the fact that he had not yet spoken to a soul, he was ever aware of the plethora of young people that surrounded him. Though he was self conscious about his age in a sea of youth, he was beginning to feel less like a fish out of water. Slowly, he was acclimating himself to an environment that initially seemed quite alien. He would never have surmised that he would find himself sitting in a classroom well beyond his final years in school. Yet, any discomfort he experienced was mitigated by thoughts of his final goal and his growing confidence that it would all be worth the effort.

Exiting the classroom, he held the door open for a classmate, the young woman who sat in front of him.

"Thank you, sir," she said, smiling at Stephen.

"You're welcome," he answered, a little taken aback at being addressed as 'sir'. He was used to it in business, but in this context, coming from so young a person, it momentarily unnerved him. He instantly knew why. He was well aware that he was older than the other students, but up until that moment he had never felt old. Now, he did.

"You sit behind me, don't you? What's your major? By the way, my name is Danielle. But only my parents call me that. Everyone else calls me Danny."

"Um...it's math...I'm going to be a math teacher," responded Stephen. A moment ago he had felt old, and now smiling to himself, he momentarily felt young. When was the last time anyone had asked his major? Twenty years ago, perhaps? "I'm Stephen, Stephen Brook."

"Hi, Stephen Brook," giggled Danny. "My major is elementary ed...second grade...can't wait."

"My wife Lila taught third grade."

"Third grade would be nice, too. Second or third," said Danny, blithely rummaging through her pocketbook in search of a piece of gum. "What do you think of the course?" she asked, pulling out two pieces and offering one to Stephen.

"Thanks," said Stephen, taking the gum. "I'm enjoying it. Especially the statistics."

"That's what I don't like," responded Danny. "It's a little too dry for me. I'd like some more practical stuff. Situations we'd experience in the classroom. More hands on."

"I can see what you mean. I spend a good part of my day with statistics. They certainly can be dry."

"What do you do?"

"I work in a bank."

"That's funny. My boyfriend does, too. He's a teller. Is that what you do?"

"Not exactly," answered Stephen, smiling. He was enjoying the conversation, finding Danny to be quite charming. "I'm the..."

"He won't be one forever, of course. Just until he finishes school," she continued, chattering away. "Who did you say teaches third grade? You did mention that? Don't mind me. I'm such a scatterbrain sometimes."

"My wife Lila did."

"Oh. Why did she stop? Did she have a baby?"

Stephen felt a sudden flash of anguish. "She passed away last spring," he said, making a great effort to hide his discomfort.

"Oh," responded Danny, uncharacteristically at a loss for words. "I'm sorry."

"Thank you. It's...it's alright."

"So how did you end up here?" asked Danny. "You know, from the bank and all..."

"I like math," said Stephen. "And kids. My friend Nat convinced me to become a teacher."

"That's a funny name," giggled Danny. "Sounds like an old person."

"He's about seventy-five," responded Stephen. "But he's anything but old," he added in Nat's defense.

"That's...that's good," responded Danny, hesitating, unsure of what to say next. She glanced at her watch. "It's almost ten minutes. Maybe we should get back in." She started to walk towards the classroom door.

"Sure," said Stephen, sensing that perhaps he had made a muddle of the conversation, dampening Danny's youthful spirit with his talk of Lila and Nat.

"It's been nice talking to you," she said, glancing behind as Stephen followed her in.

"Same here," answered Stephen, sensing too that it was unlikely he would have another conversation with her.

Upon returning to his seat, Stephen sat down and stared at the back of Danny's head, at her long flowing hair. He knew for certain that the gulf between his eyes and her hair was substantially greater than the width of a desktop. It was a lifetime. His. He laughed at himself, unreservedly. Having walked out of the classroom not yet forty, he had returned, after a few minutes talking with Danny, feeling closer to fifty. He realized too the irony of his current situation. He knew quite well that he had more in common with Nat than with a young woman perhaps fifteen years his junior. He would not wish to turn back the clock to twenty something. Either was he ready to envision himself as being seventy something. Sitting at his desk, watching now as Professor Skylar returned to the lectern, he realized that he needed to remain in the only place suitable for him, his very own present at his very own age.

❈❈

Overcome with hunger and knowing that an empty refrigerator awaited him at home, Stephen drove from the campus directly to the supermarket. After parking his car, he walked briskly toward the front entrance to the market, spying a familiar figure just ahead.

"Mind if I join you?" called Stephen.

Nat turned around at the sound of Stephen's familiar voice.

"Always enjoy your company," he smiled, waiting with his cart for Stephen to catch up.

"What brings you here, Nat? Looking for special ingredients? Cooking up something new?"

"Banana bread, pal. Ida used to make it for the kids. One way to get 'em to eat fruit. Between the sugar inside and cinnamon on top, probably never even knew they were eatin' bananas. Loved to eat it myself. Need to buy some bananas and bakin' powder. And you? Grabbin' a bite after class?"

"How'd you guess?"

"Just figured. Why don't we hustle you up some dinner first and then get what I need," he suggested.

"Sure, Nat."

As they crossed the store in the direction of cooked foods, Stephen noticed that Nat glimpsed down each aisle they passed.

"Looking for something?" he innocently asked.

"Not a thing," responded Nat, unconvincingly.

"Oh," said Stephen. "What do you think about a roast chicken for dinner tonight?"

That caught Nat's attention. "Let me pick it out," he quipped.

Stephen smiled.

Shortly, with Stephen's dinner in the cart, they again crossed the store.

"Three oughta do it," said Nat, standing in front of a display of fresh bananas.

He took a bunch and tore off three. About to put them in his cart, he heard a familiar voice.

"You and bananas appear to be inseparable," said Rose Pierce. "How are you, Nat?"

Nat looked up to see Rose approaching with her basket in hand.

"You remember my name?" he asked awkwardly, turning red. "Been a while."

"How could I forget? You certainly made an impression," she smiled.

Stephen just stood there, incredulous at the apparent familiarity between the two.

Rose looked at him warmly.

"Food shopping with your son?" she asked, turning to Nat.

"Not my son," answered Nat. "My two boys live out west." He puffed out his chest with pride, glancing at Stephen. "But he's just like one. This is my buddy, Stephen Brook."

Stephen looked at Nat with an equal amount of pride.

"I have two girls myself." Rose extended her hand. "How nice to meet you, Stephen. I'm Rose Pierce."

"Hello, Rose." Stephen was at a loss for further words. Quickly, he surmised that the usual pleasantries would be to no avail. Of no use would be, "I'm so glad to finally meet you, Nat has told me so much about you." Nor could he say, "What a pleasant surprise, I was hoping to meet you soon." Neither would fit the circumstance, for obviously thought Stephen, Nat was leading a double life.

"I was just coming to buy more bananas," continued Rose. "I need the potassium. Muscles...you know." Rose shrugged her shoulders and looked at Nat, addressing him directly. "What can you do? Age is age. You lose your spouse, then your friends one by one..." She suddenly stopped. "Oh, dear!" she exclaimed. "Listen to me carry on. I apologize. It is rude of me."

"No need to apologize," responded Nat. "I know exactly whaty're sayin'. Trust me."

"Thank you, Nat," nodded Rose, intuitively understanding what lay behind his reassurance. "So tell me, what brings you and Stephen here? The way you chased after my groceries, I can't imagine you're buying bananas out of any health concerns."

"That's for sure," said Stephen, having no idea what groceries Nat had chased but having found something to say to make amends for his rather terse greeting. "You should see him ice skate."

"Now, Stephen..." began Nat, growing embarrassed by the direction of the conversation. "Banana bread," he continued, changing its course. "Gonna bake a banana bread."

"Baking a banana bread," repeated Rose, shaking her head approvingly. "Are you a baker by profession?"

"Nope. Retired. Was in the printin' trade."

"An admirable profession," said Rose.

"Thank you," Nat responded.

Stephen stood there observing the continued exchange between Nat and Rose. He felt as if he was watching a film, one to which he had arrived late. He had apparently missed the beginning, all that had preceded his arrival. Unfortunately, as the action unfolded before his eyes, there was no one to whom he could turn to make a simple query. Nothing more nor less than, "what is going on here?"

"Well," sighed Rose, "it's been a quite a long day. I'm going to finish up and be on my way. I'm so glad we met again, Nat. It was my pleasure to meet you, Stephen."

"Would you like a ride home?" asked Stephen. "I live right over on Sycamore and Nat's on Birch."

"What a coincidence!" exclaimed Rose. "I don't live far from either of you. I'm on Chestnut. It's very sweet of you to offer, but I have my car."

"Here you go," said Nat, grabbing a bunch of bananas and handing them to Rose. "These aren't too green."

"No, not too green," smiled Rose. "At my age waiting too long for bananas to turn yellow may not be a wise thing."

Nat grinned as did Stephen.

"Well, goodnight gentlemen." Rose turned to leave.

"Goodnight," responded Nat and Stephen.

Stephen wasted no time in inquiring about what he perceived to be Nat's secret life. As they crossed the parking lot with their groceries, Stephen gently put his arm around Nat's shoulder. "So," he said, in a tone of bemused shock. "When did you plan on telling me about Rose?"

"Sorry," offered Nat, sheepishly. "Ran into her the night I got you the milk. I mean really ran into her, shopping cart and all. Knocked all her groceries down. Couldn't a been more embarrassing. Don't know why I didn't mention it. Whyd'ya think?"

"I don't know, Nat. Ask me again when I finish my psychology course," he laughed.

Nat joined him. "You shoulda seen me runnin' around that aisle. Musta been a sight."

"She seems like a very nice lady."

"Got to agree with you there, pal." Nat yawned. "I'm beat. Thanks for the ride home, Stephen. Don't mind not walkin' tonight."

"You're welcome, Nat."

Stephen pulled the car out of the lot and at the first red light, turned his eyes from the road to ask Nat one more thing. He discerned a tranquil countenance staring pensively through the windshield, out into the night. He did not ask a thing. He just smiled.

The light turned green.

❀❀

Rose Pierce placed the bananas in the fruit basket on her kitchen table. She turned out the kitchen light, walked down the few steps that led to the den, and settled into her favorite chair. It was her favorite chair not because it was the most comfortable in the house, it was not, but because the things that she surrounded herself with while ensconced in that chair brought her great joy. They were things that engaged her mind. To her left was a rectangular snack tray upon which sat a stack of paperback mysteries and daily crosswords. Already imbued with a love for words and reading, Rose found that these fed her appetite for a challenging mental puzzle. To her right, beside the lamp on a small coffee table, sat her foreign film folios. Dates, times, theatres, and reviews were all at her fingertips. She tried to see at least one film a week. In front of her, on another tray, was a neat pile of papers containing articles and tips on the game of bridge. She loved to play and did so at the local community center.

Despite aches and pains and an assortment of health concerns, Rose Pierce held fast to her independence. The death of her husband did not deter her from remaining in her home, alone. Upon Sam's death she had to quickly learn the nuances of a financial world quite alien to her as well as become acquainted with the upkeep of a house. She did both. Armed with a wry sense of humor and an even greater sense of irony, Rose met the promise of each day and persevered. Though her body might betray her, she had no such misgivings about her mind. Until she could no longer think or read, she would get up each day and get out the front door of her home.

Her daughters brought her great comfort as did her small circle of remaining friends. She was a self described fatalist and accepted without fear the inevitability of her own death just as she had to accept the continued demise of her contemporaries. She did not let time slip through her fingers. An appreciation of its fleeting quality impressed her with the desire to try and fully grasp each moment and wring from it something good and fulfilling, if not for herself then for others. From her chair she supported countless charities, sending off checks that she hoped would someday translate into hope or a cure for someone's ailment. Rose Pierce, throughout her adult life, had always tried to simply be an ethical person in what she viewed as an increasingly complex world of less and less moral certitude.

Sitting tranquilly in her favorite chair that night, she did not immediately reach for a book or crossword. Instead, she let her mind drift to the produce section of the supermarket and the little man whom she had met there. Twice now she had met him in the market, and twice he had brought a smile to her face. A nice man, thought Rose. She recalled the evening's conversation and the fact that he had two sons and lived on Birch Road. Hmm...she wondered to herself, if we're about the same age, perhaps his children and my girls went to school together. Perhaps our paths have even crossed somewhere in the past at some community event...perhaps... Rose closed her eyes and mused about the possibilities of a different kind of puzzle. She nodded off to sleep.

Shortly, she was startled, awakened by the ringing of her telephone. Groggy eyed and momentarily disoriented, she was unable to rouse herself before the answering machine went on.

"Rosie? Are you there? It's me, Dora. Rosie?"

Rose got her bearings, realizing that she had left the phone in the kitchen when ordinarily she would have bought it with her to the den.

"I'll call back again," said Dora, her voice fading, as though she was no longer talking into the receiver, but to herself.

She hung up.

Rose got up from her chair. "Better call her right away," she said aloud, her voice reflecting a modicum of unease. "She'll worry."

Not yet fully awake, Rose ascended the few steps to the kitchen holding onto the wrought iron banister.

"Hi, Dora," she yawned into the phone, addressing her best friend.

"Sorry, Rosie. Did I wake you?"

"Don't pay it any mind. Just dozing. It was a busy night, food shopping and..." Rose yawned a second time.

"And what?" asked Dora.

"Oh, nothing," responded Rose.

"Rosie," countered Dora, forcefully. "Out with it."

"Well…I met an interesting gentleman in the supermarket tonight. The second time actually. The first time we sort of ran into each other, literally."

"Single?" asked Dora.

"I think so," laughed Rose, now fully awake. "Whether or not," she continued, "he seems like a good person, quite sweet."

"The good ones are already dead, Rosie. The ones that are left, well…" Dora sighed into the phone.

Rose laughed again, heartily. One of the things she loved most about Dora was her candor, her ability to say, with forthrightness and honesty, whatever was on her mind. For Rose, Dora was a refreshing respite from her own disposition to measure her words carefully, after first letting her thoughts fully crystallize. "Perhaps not every good one is dead," she answered.

"Ah…think you've found a live one! God bless you. What's his name?"

"Nat, Nat Zeigler."

"The name doesn't ring a bell. From the neighborhood?"

"He lives on Birch."

"We'll have to do a little investigating. A real live mystery for you."

"Dora!" responded Rose, firmly.

"Alright. Just keep me informed."

"There's really nothing much to tell," said Rose.

"Well, it's getting late, so maybe at bridge you can fill me in on what happened"

"Absolutely."

"Goodnight, Rosie."

"Goodnight."

After hanging up the receiver, Rose returned to the den, quite expecting to read a little bit before bed. Once settled in her chair, she quickly fell asleep instead.

The Cemetery

STEPHEN TURNED THE WHEEL AND the car slowly passed the open, wrought iron gates of Oakwood Cemetery. As the car progressed along the narrow roadway, Nat pointed up ahead.

"There, pal. Over on the right. That's the office. Pull up by the curb."

Stephen eased the car to the right as the road transformed into the shape of a circle with the office situated along a portion of its arc. He pulled up in front of the office.

"Listen," said Nat, turning to Stephen. "I know this isn't the place you'd wanna be, what with everything still so fresh in your mind. So, I just wanna thank you again for agreein' to come along with..."

"Don't say another word," interrupted Stephen. "You asked, Nat." He paused and then definitively added, "It was my choice."

"Sure you're alright?"

"Just tell me where to go." Stephen's voice relinquished its decisive tone for one of earnest inquiry. "Are you alright?" he asked, gently gripping Nat's shoulder and placing added emphasis on the word 'you'.

"I'm o.k., pal." Nat inhaled deeply. "Just follow the circle out to the right and then go straight up the road. Like we discussed, I need to talk to Ida...direct."

"You got it, Nat." Stephen pulled the car from the curb.

⁂

They passed row upon row of gravestones.

"Should come more often," lamented Nat, as they continued along. "A little further," he added, stone faced.

Stephen sat silently, simply waiting for Nat to tell him when to stop.

Nat suddenly did.

"This is it, pal. Just pull over anywhere."

Stephen eased the car to the right and parked.

Nat got out, pulled his coat collar up and put on his hat. He waited for Stephen to join him.

"Just lead the way," said Stephen.

Nat put his hands in his pockets and drew his arms tightly to his sides. "It's right over here," he responded with a nod.

He walked solemnly amidst the monuments, treading familiar ground. With Stephen by his side, he abruptly came to a standstill. He took off his hat.

Stephen stared down at the footstone not far from his own feet. Ida's name stared back at him, as did the dates that acted as bookends, marking the beginning and end to her story. Below those two dates were four words signifying the life of Ida Zeigler as seen through the eyes of those she left behind. "Beloved wife, mother, grandmother." Stephen turned to Nat in time to witness a countenance slowly becoming suffused with the warm glow of memory.

Nat stared straight ahead, his eyes moist.

Sensing that his presence was for the moment superfluous, Stephen quietly took a step back.

Nat did not notice.

Stephen spied a narrow marble bench nestled between two yews, a few paces directly behind Nat. He receded there and sat down.

With his hat dangling from his fingertips and his hands clasped behind his back, Nat inhaled deeply.

"Ida...it's me..." He faltered for an instant. "The boys... they're just fine. You'd be awful proud of 'em. Grandkids too." Nat wavered and momentarily looked skyward.

Stephen, from where he sat, could only see the back of Nat. He could hear each word spoken, but could only imagine the array of emotion displayed on Nat's face. He watched as Nat's head tilted upward and then his eyes were drawn to the hat.

With his fingertips, Nat began to gently pull his hat by the brim in a circular motion. It slowly rotated behind his back, passing through his fingers.

Stephen watched, hypnotically.

"Ida..." Nat regained his voice, his head pointed to the ground.

Stephen was startled to attention.

"You've always been my best gal..." continued Nat, reaching deep into his heart, despite holding his hat. "Fact is, you're my only gal and always will be." He began to sway ever so slightly from side to side and just barely shifted his feet.

Stephen noticed and sensed that perhaps Nat was trying somehow to gain a firmer foothold on a world that was perhaps shifting under him.

"There's a little lady, Ida. Name's Rose. Don't really know 'er, but...I...I maybe wouldn't mind a little company. Been alone a long time, Ida. No guarantee anyone would wanna spend time with an old fella like me but...who knows. Not much makin' sense anymore anyhow."

Stephen saw Nat's feet now firmly planted and the hat immobile.

"Gonna ask to see'er. Nothin' serious." Nat paused, and with his eyes closed, nodded his head up and down. "Remember Ida, in my book you're always number one." He put his hat on, opened his eyes and rubbed them, taking perhaps the deepest breath of his long life. Suddenly, he remembered Stephen and quickly turned to his left.

"Over here," called Stephen.

Nat turned around. "Been sittin' the whole time?"

"Waiting for you, pal."

Nat walked over and sat beside Stephen.

"Thanks, Stephen. Appreciate your comin' along and keepin' me company."

"Are you alright?"

Nat pursed his lips and shook his head from side to side. "What can I say? I always kept things fair and square with my Ida and now's no different...I hope she hears me."

"You're a good man, Nat. I'm sure Ida heard every word you said."

"You know, pal, I gotta tell ya something. It's a funny thing to be sayin' considerin' where we're sittin', but you and me, we're two lucky fellas."

"I know what you're going to say," responded Stephen with a slow, measured nod of his head. "And yes," he added wryly while taking a quick look around, "this is an odd place to talk about our luck."

Nat smiled. "We were blessed with two beautiful little ladies. Darn good marriages. Nothin' to sneeze at in this crazy world. Yep, we're two lucky fellas, Stephen. That's one thing for sure even if nothin' else makes much sense in the big scheme a things."

"As a matter of fact, Nat, I've been thinking a lot about the big picture since…"

"Nothin' unusual 'bout that. Just gotta be careful, buddy. Bein' alone and thinkin' can lead ya right down some dark roads sometimes. Keep an eye on that thinkin'."

"I appreciate the advice," said Stephen, shaking his head with approval. "I'll try not to let my mind get too carried away."

"Sounds good. Now what's the story with this big picture?"

"Actually, Nat, there really isn't a big picture. There's a lot of little ones." Stephen paused. "Some we choose, but most of them are random and unplanned. In the end though, it all just may make perfect sense."

Nat stared at Stephen, mystified. He scratched his head in bewilderment and while doing so, inadvertently struck the brim of his hat with his knuckles, pushing it up and forward on his head. The front brim now overshadowed his brow. He pushed his hat back up, uncovered his eyes and peered at Stephen. "You lost me after the word actually, buddy," he said with a grin.

"Listen, Nat," said Stephen in earnest, "the night that you were caught out in the snow, it was Lila who saw you from the window. We had just finished cleaning the dinner dishes and were sitting at the kitchen table talking when she said that she thought she heard a noise. I told her it was probably just the wind. I don't to this day know what it is she heard. It couldn't have been you. Not from outside. The next thing I know, she leaves the kitchen and is calling me from the living room to hurry up, there's someone out in the snow who needs help."

"Your Lila was always lookin' out for me," interjected Nat. "Right from the beginning."

"That's just it, Nat," Stephen quickly rejoined. "If it hadn't been for Lila, we wouldn't be sitting here today. Maybe I passed you or even Ida on the street hundreds of times. Maybe you passed by Lila dozens of times over the years. And then one night, one seemingly random event, and here we are sitting together in a cemetery!"

Nat looked at Stephen pensively, slowly marshalling all of his faculties and deliberating. "So!" he finally exclaimed, "if I've got this straight, maybe I passed by Rose Pierce who knows how many times in the supermarket or the neighborhood last couple a years, but if I didn't forget the applesauce and go back for it, I never woulda met 'er."

"Maybe not," said Stephen, "and that's just it. One seemingly haphazard event can change your life and then lead to another and another. You wouldn't have been in the supermarket that night if I had had onions in the house."

"I'm stayin' with ya on this, Stephen, but how's this all make perfect sense in the end?"

"You know as well as I, Nat, nobody can predict the future. But if you take one random event after another and link them all together, they can only lead you to one place."

"Where you were meant to be," said Nat, his words imbued with certainty, his eyes ablaze with understanding.

"Yes, your fate," added Stephen, definitively.

Nat's newfound understanding quickly changed to perplexity. He scratched his head in bewilderment a second time. Again, his hat tipped forward on his head. He pushed it back up and looked at Stephen, quizzically. "Where does it begin?" he asked.

"Where does what begin?" responded Stephen.

"The whole thing. Where d'ya put your finger on the startin' point. The first thing leadin' ya to where ya belong."

Now Stephen scratched his head. "That's a heck of a question, Nat. I'm not so sure of that. I guess...anywhere."

"Hmm...anywhere. Gotta think on that."

"How about another day for that one," suggested Stephen. "It's getting late."

"A bit done in myself, pal. We'll chew on that one another time."

They stood up simultaneously.

"Well, Ida," began Nat, taking a few steps forward.

Stephen accompanied him.

"Time for me and my pal Stephen to go. Like I said to him, Ida... me and him, we're some lucky fellas. Two beautiful wives. Wonderful years for each of us. Life don't stop, Ida. I learned that. And appreciatin' the past and what we had...that don't stop either." Nat's voice faltered.

Stephen put his arm around Nat's shoulder.

A few fragile rays of waning sunlight suddenly streamed through the cloudy skies, falling at their feet.

Nat peered up towards the sky and then, turning his eyes to the ground, smiled and winked.

"I'm gonna take that as a sign, Ida." Turning to Stephen, he asked, "What d'ya think, pal?"

"No doubt about it," smiled Stephen. "She's a gem, Nat."

"Thanks, buddy. I'm ready to go."

❄❄

They walked to the car in silence and passed back through the wrought iron gates lost in their own thoughts.

A short distance from the cemetery, Nat's thoughts crystallized into words.

"You know, considerin' what you were sayin', there's no tellin' what might be in store for you just waitin' around the next corner."

"You're right," said Stephen. "It's crossed my mind. You never know. We'll have to just wait and see."

"In the meantime, pal, whenever you want to visit…"

"I know you'd come along."

"Can always count on me, Stephen."

A Single Red Rose

"THOUGHT I WAS TALLER THAN that," grumbled Nat, staring at his reflection in the full length bed room mirror. "Must be shrinkin'."

Aside from his morning shave, Nat had not had any inclination to gaze at himself in a mirror over these past few years. And even then, pulling the razor across his face never gave rise to studying his features, but was simply a daily chore that if not for the risk of physical harm, he could have done with his eyes closed. With his eyes now wide open, he fully surveyed the man in the mirror. "The mirror don't lie, I guess." He watched himself shrug his shoulders. "Sure coulda sworn I was taller." A smile crept across his face. "Too late t'grow, I guess."

He stared intently at his face and ran the palm of his hand over his cheeks. "Not too rough," he mused aloud, "not for an old man." He nodded with satisfaction. "Not too wrinkled, either."

❈❈

Nat bounded down his front steps with the alacrity of a man seemingly on his way to cash in a winning lottery ticket. Only he was seeking a more valuable prize, predicated on a much bigger gamble than the wager of a dollar. For a man who had spent forty-five years assiduously adhering to a daily work routine and four years to a daily dinner routine, he was wantonly throwing caution way beyond his grasp in the hope of simply running into Rose Pierce. He had neither a shopping list in hand nor a plan in mind as he headed towards the supermarket. He only possessed a vague sense that this might be unlike any shopping expedition he had ever gone on.

In no time at all, he found himself standing adjacent to the bananas, across from the cucumbers. Wishing to meet Rose and hoping that her desire for potassium would draw her to the bananas, he waited patiently there. He stood with his hat in hand, holding it behind his back and tapping it methodically against his body. His right foot tapped in concert with his hat.

Periodically he stepped just slightly to the right, or to the left as need be, allowing people to pass by and reach the bananas. He continually scoured the supermarket, as far as his eyes could see, awaiting her appearance. Suddenly, he stopped searching and focused directly on the little flower market situated at the front entrance.

"Why not?" he asked himself, already beginning to walk in that direction. "No harm in bein' a sport," he answered himself.

He reached the flowers and slowly walked around the carousel, reading the labels on the steel pails.

"Carnations, mums, roses, daisies, mixed bouquet..."

He stopped in front of the pail containing single, wrapped roses, and momentarily hesitated. Overtaken by more than a modicum of self-consciousness, he looked first to his left and then to his right before grabbing a red rose.

"Pay for it later, I guess," he said under his breath.

Now he stood, waiting impatiently with a rose in one hand and his hat in the other, tapping his foot and staring towards the front entrance of the supermarket. Tapping and staring as a steady stream of people walked in, one after another, but not one that he recognized. With his eyes riveted ahead, he had become oblivious to his surroundings. Oblivious until the arrival not of Rose Pierce, but of self-doubt.

"Who'm I tryin' to kid?" he finally asked himself, dispirited, his voice barely audible. "An old man standin' in the middle of the supermarket waitin', holdin' a flower. Must look awful silly," he muttered. Unfortunately, with a glance to his left and then right, he realized that his instincts were correct.

It was he who was being stared at, by other shoppers.

"Starin' at the silly old man with the rose talkin' to himself," he mumbled. "Don't blame ya."

Nat dropped the rose back into its bucket and put his hat on, somewhat askew. Without so much as adjusting it properly, he looked down at the floor and slunk out of the supermarket.

❈❈

After a restless night fraught with feelings of disappointment at Rose's failure to appear and self administered reproaches for his own foolishness in assuming she would, Nat awakened early, exhausted. He rubbed his eyes.

"Could use a hot cup of coffee," he grumbled, slowly getting out of bed and dragging himself to the kitchen.

He opened the refrigerator door and gazed inside, again rubbing his eyes. "No coffee. Not even milk. Shoulda gone with a shoppin' list yesterday. Never mind roses. Gotta get my head outa the clouds."

He washed and shaved and dressed, listlessly.

Plodding along with little energy, bound this time to simply purchase mundane necessities, Nat walked back to the supermarket.

Upon entering the familiar doors, he trod towards the coffee section, having to pass by the flower carousel. He stopped momentarily beside the bucket of roses. Carelessly pulling one out, he shook his head from side to side.

"Musta been outa my mind ta think..."

"Such a beautiful rose," said a familiar voice. "Are you an admirer of flowers?"

Nat looked up to see Rose standing in front of him. "Well... I...I", he stammered, startled. "Here it's...for you," he said in a tremulous voice, awkwardly thrusting the rose towards her as he tried to regain some semblance of composure.

❦❦

Now Rose Pierce was startled. Never could she have imagined a greeting such as this upon entering the neighborhood supermarket. Standing immobile and dumbfounded, her face turned a bright red.

"Why thank you, Nat," she responded, breathless and embarrassed. "It's so sweet of you."

"Pleasure," whispered Nat, the previous night's disappointment fading as Rose's smile appeared.

"I quite honestly don't know what to say," continued Rose. "Such an unexpected surprise."

"Surprised myself," whispered Nat, beneath his breath.

Rose did not hear him. She had grasped the stem and brought the flower to her nose, inhaling deeply. "Lovely, just lovely. Here." She stuck the rose under Nat's nose.

"Smells good," said Nat.

Rose smiled.

Nat followed suit.

"Coffee," Nat suddenly muttered, with the rose still under his nose. The ability to speak a complete sentence had apparently evaded him.

"Did you say coffee, Nat?"

Nat hesitated for a moment. "Would ya like to go for a cup a coffee with me sometime?" he asked, finally able to string together a number of words.

"Oh, my! You're just full of surprises. I would like that."

"It's a deal then?" asked Nat, beginning to shed a burden so unfamiliar to a creature of habit, the weight of uncertainty.

"A deal it is," smiled Rose.

"Good," Nat nodded.

"If you could hold this and just give me a second," said Rose, letting go of the stem as Nat grasped it. She subsequently opened her pocketbook and reaching in, took out a small booklet and a pencil.

Nat watched quietly as she thumbed through the pages.

"Here we are," she finally said.

Nat could see the boxes on the page and that words filled each one.

"Friday," said Rose. "Would Friday be alright? I have a bridge game at ten fifteen and could meet you earlier."

Nat hadn't a calendar to check.

"Friday's good," he answered, his voice now steady and more fluid, reflecting a growing sense of ease. "D'ya know the old restaurant on Tulip Avenue? Next to the stationery store."

"I do," responded Rose. "But I don't think they call them stationery stores anymore."

"Everythings changin'," laughed Nat.

"Yes, everything is changing," agreed Rose. "What time would you like to meet?"

"Nine o.k.?"

"Nine it is."

Nat watched as Rose wrote.

After writing, "coffee with Nat 9:00", she put the calendar and pencil back in her bag.

Nat gave her back the rose.

A few seconds of silence lingered in the air between them.

"Well," said Rose, "Friday for coffee it is then. I guess I should do my shopping."

"Yes, your shoppin'," echoed Nat. "I oughta be goin'."

"Thank you again, Nat."

"My pleasure."

Nat walked towards the front entrance, his eyes closing for an instant as a smile crossed his lips.

Rose walked towards the bananas, clutching one item that she knew for a fact had not been on her shopping list.

❄❄

Nat traversed the streets leading home with a lighthearted, contented feeling, replaying in his mind's eye all that had just transpired. Suddenly, within a block of his house, he stopped short.

"Geez!" he exclaimed aloud, tapping himself on the forehead with the palm of his hand. "I didn't get what I went for! No coffee. No milk." He threw up his arms, hands empty.

"Holy...the rose. I didn't pay for the rose! The little lady's gonna have to pay for her own flower! Some sport you are, Nat Zeigler!"

Nat turned around, as if he expected to see all the way back to the supermarket. He thought for a moment and considered going back.

"Shouldn't do that," he said to a deserted street. "Walk back in and she'll think I'm crazier than she already thinks. Best t'leave it alone. Next thing you know she'll be payin' for her own coffee Friday mornin'."

He shook his head from side to side, glanced up at the sky, and continued on.

Not two doors from his own, he was startled to hear his name ring out.

"Nat! Nat Zeigler! Up here!"

He stopped in his tracks. Though the voice seemed familiar, he was stunned at the sound of his very own name resounding along the street that he had so often tread in silence these many years. He looked up, to his left at first and then to his right, scanning the houses across the way. Halfway up a double hung ladder which leaned against a brick tudor, grasping a rung with one hand and waving towards Nat with the other, was a slight, gray haired man.

"Hey, Gus. You alright?" called Nat, with alarm, instantly recognizing his longtime neighbor.

"Fine, Nat. I'm perfectly fine," called back Gus. "Don't worry. Could use a hand though if you have a minute."

"Sure thing, Gus. On my way."

Nat crossed the street and as he walked across Gus's lawn, he took in the sight of the unlit Christmas lights adorning the façade of Gus's house. He approached the foot of the ladder and looked up.

"Thanks for coming over, Nat," said Gus. "Good to see you. It's been a while. Don't see much of anyone anymore. Especially in winter."

"No, not like the old days, Gus. Everyone locked away inside if they're still…"

"Know what you mean," sighed Gus.

"How's Betty?" asked Nat.

"She's fine," answered Gus. "Thanks for asking. And you, Nat, how are you?"

"Still got some life left in me. Still kickin'. So what can I do for ya?"

"If you could just steady the ladder for me for a few minutes. I have to go up another rung or two to finish up this last row. Not as sure footed as I used to be."

"Sure thing, Gus."

Nat gripped either side of the ladder and leaned into it with as much strength as he could muster.

"Another season comin' up," he said. "House looks good."

"Thanks, Nat. I try."

"Ya do more than try."

"Just about done. Be down in a second."

"Take your time, Gus."

"One last…there that's it. I think we're in business."

Gus began to descend the ladder.

Nat stepped away as Gus's feet approached the top of his hat.

Within moments the two men were standing side by side.

Gus took a few steps back.

Nat followed suit.

"Looks all set," said Gus.

Nat noted the apparent satisfaction in his voice.

"I'm glad you do this every year, Gus," said Nat, nodding his head with approval.

"Why thank you, Nat," beamed Gus. "How would you like to do me one more favor?"

"Just name it."

Gus pointed to the ground just to the left of the ladder. "Grab the end of those two electric cords lying there, plug them together, and light her up!"

"Are you... sure?" stammered Nat, in disbelief. "Don't you wanna do that?"

"Give it a go," answered Gus, winking.

Nat hesitated a moment, and then as if propelled from behind, sprung to the ladder, grabbed the two cords and pushed them together. He quickly turned around to see the glee on Gus's face, took a few steps forward, and then turned again to face the house.

"Geez!" he exclaimed.

"Merry Christmas," smiled Gus, extending his hand to Nat.

Nat looked at Gus. "Merry Christmas," he whispered, grabbing Gus's hand.

"Listen, Nat. It's just me and Betty now. We're all getting on in years. No sense being alone. Join us for Christmas dinner this year. I know Betty would love it."

"Well...I...I...Thank you, but..."

"Don't have to answer right away," added Gus. "You let us know."

Nat crossed over to his side of the street in deep thought. Upon reaching his front porch, he momentarily turned and glanced at the brightly lit house. "Hmm...," he exhaled, "why didn't I think a that?" Looking down at his empty hands, he began to count on his right hand fingers, one by one, using his left forefinger. "There's Stephen," he began excitedly, tapping his right pinky first. "Then there's Rose," he continued, tapping his next finger. "And maybe the kids would come...Betty and Gus...why not...Christmas dinner at my house...Ida'd be proud...Maybe can't pull it off this year...if not, next...could cook up a storm..." Nat stopped to catch his breath. "I'm all done in," he sighed. "Too much excitement this mornin'. Gettin' a little ahead of myself. Maybe use a nap."

Nat entered the house and was fast asleep in no time at all.

A Deal Is A Deal

As Stephen Brook turned the corner onto Tulip Avenue, he glanced at his watch. The hands read eight fifty-eight. Stephen walked past the florist shop, bakery, and stationery store before coming to a standstill in front of the restaurant. He stared through the front window, searchingly.

From the opposite direction, Rose Pierce turned the corner onto Tulip Avenue. As she approached the restaurant, she spied a young man staring into its window. Peering through her glasses at the side of his face, she thought she recognized Nat's friend, Stephen, whom she had met at the supermarket. A few steps further and she arrived at the restaurant.

Stephen, not finding what he had sought, suddenly turned in her direction.

Rose instantly experienced a twofold realization accompanied by a single flash of overwhelming dread. Yes, it was Stephen, Nat's friend, and something unexpected and terrible must have happened to Nat. There could be no other explanation for Stephen's presence in Nat's stead. In the circles she traveled, sudden absence only meant one thing. She looked beseechingly at Stephen as her heart began to sink.

Stephen looked at Rose and in that same instant read in her face the tale she had instinctively told herself.

"He's fine. Nothing bad happened," he whispered reassuringly. "Trust me. He just couldn't come today and a deal is a deal. That's what he said. He sent me." Stephen said as much as he could in one breath in order to quickly dispel Rose's fears.

As the color returned to her face, Rose took a deep breath. "He hasn't been ill, has he?" she asked, plaintively.

"No, no, not at all," responded Stephen. "His daughter-in-law's father passed away suddenly and Nat flew out to Arizona for the funeral." Stephen paused as he opened the door to the restaurant. "Please come inside from the cold," he continued. "I'll tell you whatever you'd like to know, over a cup of coffee. I have express orders from the boss!"

Rose smiled, entering the restaurant on the heels of Stephen's reassurances.

Without even waiting for someone to approach, Stephen unhesitatingly directed Rose to the table where he, Lila, and Nat had once sat together.

"You've eaten here before?" asked Rose.

Stephen felt a quick stab of anguish. "Yes," he simply answered.

"Oh," said Rose, taking off her hat and coat.

Stephen pulled out a chair for her.

"Such a gentleman," she said.

He took the seat opposite her.

A waiter approached and handed each of them a menu.

"Can I get you coffee to start?" he asked.

"Rose?" asked Stephen.

"Decaf, please."

"I'll have regular," answered Stephen.

The waiter walked away.

"Nat said to order anything you'd like," said Stephen. "His treat."

"That's very kind of him. This must have all happened very suddenly. What a difficult time for a family. Dear me."

"Very sudden," nodded Stephen, his voice barely audible. "It's awfully hard," he added, his words marked by a hint of melancholy.

Rose took note of his tone and glancing at him over the top of her menu, quickly sensed that perhaps he had experienced a sudden, unexpected loss of his own.

"Nat had no way of reaching you," continued Stephen, reclaiming his normal tone of voice.

"He first got a call yesterday morning and he didn't want you to come here and not find him here. That's where I come into the picture." Stephen smiled.

Rose was glad that he smiled, dispelling her previous thought.

"Well, what would you like, Rose?" asked Stephen.

"A muffin would be fine. Bran."

"That's all?" inquired Stephen. "Nat would probably insist you order more. He enjoys treating."

"Ice skating too, I gather."

"You remember what I said in the supermarket. You have a good memory."

"Thank you, Stephen. I try and keep my mind sharp. There's just so..."

The waiter appeared to take their order.

"What were you saying, Rose?" asked Stephen, upon the waiter's departure. "You didn't finish your sentence."

"Just that I try and keep my mind engaged. There's just so much I can do physically, at least I can keep my mind active. I've always been like that, though. I guess I'm a thinker and not so much a doer."

"So am I," agreed Stephen, firmly.

"Your friend Nat, now that's a different story," laughed Rose. "Ice skating, baking, shopping...I'm sure there's more. There is a man on the go!"

"No stopping him," said Stephen, throwing up his arms, feigning exasperation.

"We are who we are," offered Rose. "Whether a thinker or doer. You must be true to yourself." She paused for a moment. "I'm sorry. It sounds like I'm dispensing advice. I don't mean to."

"No, you're absolutely right." Stephen stiffened and nodded his head up and down. "My wife was true to herself. All the time."

The waiter returned with their order, Rose's bran muffin and a corn muffin for Stephen.

Before the waiter had even turned to leave, Rose realized that her instincts about Stephen's past had been correct.

"I'm so sorry," she said.

"Thank you," Stephen whispered.

"What was her name? I'll bet she was an angel."

"She was. Her name was Lila."

"What a lovely name. How did you both...?" Rose stopped before she completed her sentence. "I apologize again," she said. "I don't mean to pry."

"You're not. Meet? It is a lovely name, isn't it?"

"Yes to both," answered Rose, relieved that Stephen was not offended.

"At summer camp when we were teenagers. Working with children."

"Teenagers," repeated Rose. "So young."

Stephen took a sip of coffee.

"Sam and I met when we were young also," mused Rose, staring into her cup for a few seconds, absentmindedly stirring the coffee with a spoon. "Though not as young as you and your Lila," she added, looking up.

"How did you meet?" asked Stephen. "Now it's me who's prying."

Rose smiled. "Such a night. So long ago." She paused, sighing.

In that pause, Stephen watched as Rose's smile and bright eyes evinced the warm glow of remembrance. He recognized that look, having seen it on Nat's face whenever Nat retrieved a fond memory of Ida.

"At a dance," continued Rose, wistfully. "We only danced with each other. Not another partner. Sam swept me off my feet," she laughed. "I guess I've always been a romantic at heart, despite life's lessons."

"Life's lessons," repeated Stephen. "I really like the way you put that, Rose."

"I've certainly had my share as I'm sure you have. The key though is to learn from them." Rose shook her head from side to side and again stared into her cup. "I only wish my Victoria would," she continued, momentarily dispirited. "If you don't learn from your mistakes, you'll just keep repeating them."

Stephen assumed that Victoria was Rose's daughter.

Rose looked up at him. "I'm sorry. Victoria is my daughter. The wayward one." The hint of a smile returned to her face. "I like to call her that. She doesn't mind."

"You have two daughters, don't you?"

"Ah, you've a good memory, too. Victoria and Elizabeth, the two bright stars in my life. They're a blessing."

"That's just what Nat would say about his two sons. No doubt about it."

"I'm sure he would. The children are certainly a blessing, especially now at my age. I'm sure he feels the same way about his sons. Though, I do fret about Victoria. How I wish she would settle down."

Stephen felt a quick twinge of sadness, resulting from the sudden thought of his old age, perhaps devoid of such a blessing.

It quickly passed, effaced by the sudden sight of Rose throwing up her arms in mock despair.

"But you can't control everything," she exclaimed. "Now that's a lesson to learn. But if you do learn it, there's no guarantee you'll always be able to practice it."

"There's no guarantee with anything," added Stephen, "especially the idea that things will last forever."

He took another sip of coffee.

Rose looked at him as she picked at her bran muffin. To her, Stephen's eyes matched the gravity of his words, for in those eyes she recognized both weariness and wisdom beyond his years. She usually only saw that in the eyes of her contemporaries. At his age she surmised, she was simply raising her daughters, her gaze reflecting nothing more than their images.

"Would you like something else to eat?" Stephen asked. "Nat's treat," he reiterated.

Rose laughed. "No, thank you. You and Nat must be old friends. Just the way you talk about him and the way you seemed together. It's good to care about someone and have someone care about you."

"Yes, it is," said Stephen. "We're not such old friends, though. We met less than a year ago."

"I'm surprised," responded Rose.

"It was an odd occurrence," offered Stephen.

"Could it have been odder than mine?" countered Rose.

"Probably a toss-up. Nat was walking home in a snowstorm and took the wrong fork. He exhausted himself and literally came to a stop right in front of our house. If Lila hadn't seen him from the window...I hate to think..."

Rose threw up her arms in bewilderment. The second time they had gone flying up. "It's a funny world, Stephen. Don't you think? You meet Nat the way you did, and me, I happen to be right in the condiment aisle when he comes racing around the corner...and now here I am sitting in a restaurant having a bran muffin...and...we just never know what's on the horizon and where it will lead."

"No, we don't," smiled Stephen. "We surely don't."

"Oh, dear me!" exclaimed Rose, glancing at her watch. "Just look at the time. I have a bridge game at ten fifteen. My, how the time has gone by."

"And I should be getting to work," said Stephen. "I'll ask for the check."

"Thank you, Stephen. You will thank Nat for me."

"Of course."

Standing at the counter, with his wallet still open, Stephen suddenly turned to Rose. "I almost forgot," he exclaimed. "Here, this is for you." He reached into his wallet and took out two dollars. "Nat told me not to forget."

Rose was confounded.

"The flower," said Stephen.

"Oh!" Rose reached into her bag and took out a change purse. She opened it. "Here," she said, with a smile from ear to ear. "It was a dollar fifty." She took out two quarters.

Stephen just shook his head as she placed the quarters in his hand.

He held the door open for Rose as they exited the restaurant, parting company on Tulip Avenue.

"Good-bye, Stephen. Thank you again. And Nat."

"You're welcome. Enjoy your bridge game."

✻✻

As Rose walked towards the corner, she reflected on her unantici-pated breakfast with Nat's friend. She had enjoyed the morning's conversation, noting to herself how well spoken her breakfast companion was. What a pleasant young man, she mused. She wondered about his allusion to his wife. Such a terrible thing, she thought to herself. As if there isn't enough tragedy in this world. Rose crossed the street and suddenly thought about her daughter. "If only Victoria could meet a thoughtful, stable man like that," she pondered aloud.

Suddenly, she felt a trifle anxious. As the community center loomed ahead, rising above the surrounding homes and coming in sight, she remembered the early morning phone call she had received. Dora was sick and could not join her today. Rose would have to play with another bridge partner. Nat, Stephen, Lila, Victoria, breakfast, flowers…all faded from view as she contemplated the morning with a strange partner.

❀❀

It came as no surprise to Stephen when early that evening, his phone rang.

"Well, pal. What's the good word from New York?" asked Nat, from across the continent.

Stephen had no doubt what Nat wanted to know. "It all went well," he answered. "I took care of everything for you. She's lovely, Nat. Very bright, thoughtful, and quite a sense of humor. Your luck is holding out. But listen, how are you? You had me worried there right before you left."

"Guess it's a good sign she showed up," said Nat, not yet ready for the conversation to change course.

Stephen chuckled. "Couldn't have asked for a better sign, pal. She's certainly interested by the likes of our conversation."

Nat's sense of relief at this bit of news was palpable to Stephen, even from a distance of perhaps two thousand miles.

"Whew!" exclaimed Nat. "Good to hear that."

"Stop worrying about what's going on here and try to enjoy your family while you can. And...you still haven't told me how you are."

"I did alright, buddy. Took good care a me on that plane. Sorry to worry ya. What can I say? After sittin' in my chair for four years, it's been one new thing after another. And goin' to the airport, let alone flyin' across the country...long way from the neighborhood...who'd a ever figured...had me a little rattled...

but you know as well as me, Stephen, gotta do the right thing no matter how tough. Had ta be here."

"I know."

"And how are you doin'?"

"I'm...fine," answered Stephen, a slight hesitation in his voice. Nat didn't notice. "A little touch 'n go out here, but I'll fill ya in when I get home. Don't forget Tuesday night. Glad everything went well at breakfast."

"Not a hitch."

"Take care of the flower?"

"Taken care of."

"I appreciate it, Stephen. That's a big favor ya did for me. I won't forget."

"I know you won't, Nat."

"Listen, pal. I oughta say good-bye. Callin' long distance I don't wanna run up the kid's phone bill."

"I understand." Stephen was sure Nat's son wouldn't mind his father talking longer, but he acquiesced to Nat's wishes nonetheless. "I'll see you when you get home."

"Thanks again for holdin' the fort while I'm gone."

"No problem. Just have a safe trip home."

"Will do, pal."

Stephen hung up the phone and contemplated the long weekend ahead.

The Road Ahead

STEPHEN PULLED UP IN FRONT of the arrival's terminal, turned off the ignition and settled back in his seat, awaiting Nat's appearance. While gazing at the countless people bustling to and fro, he smiled to himself with wonder and a considerable amount of disbelief, knowing that he had been amongst a similar throng just the night before.

Within an hour after parting from Rose last Friday morning and arriving at the bank, he had received a telephone call that precipitated a weekend of anticipation and anxiety, not to mention a Monday trip to Boston. George Aarons, district manager for the northeast and Stephen's direct superior had telephoned from the corporate office in Boston. Stephen, having picked up the receiver, fully expected to hear the voice of Mr. Miles, ever in need of reassurance, which Stephen was happy to provide, concerning his retirement portfolio. Instead, it was George Aarons.

"Hello, Stephen. How are you?"

Stephen recognized George's voice immediately.

"Doing the best I can, George."

"All any of us can do, Stephen. You know, Viv and I worry about you."

"Thank you, George. I can't complain. I mean I could..." Stephen laughed. "But I won't..." He paused a moment and when George did not respond, he asked, "How are you and Vivian?"

"Vivian is well. But listen, Stephen, we need you to come up to Boston on Monday. Everything is arranged. A flight up, a return flight Monday evening. Mr. Sutton needs to speak with you. Eleven o'clock Monday morning. Stephen, it's about a promotion. Can you do it?"

Stephen sat, dumbfounded. A promotion? When? To where? He had spoken with George innumerable times over the years, yet had never heard such urgency in his voice. Whether in person or over the phone, George Aarons always spoke in a deliberative voice, marked by a mixture of genuine sincerity and no small dose of small talk. Not so today. To Stephen's surprise it was all business, direct and succinct. Stephen felt compelled to simply respond in kind.

"I'll be there, George."

"Good. A car will pick you up at Logan. My secretary will call you later this afternoon with all the details. I'll see you at the meeting."

"Thanks, George." Stephen didn't know what else to say. The conversation seemed to be at an end. He hung up the phone, perplexed, sensing that something was amiss. He certainly hadn't received any bad news, yet such a cursory conversation with George concerning potentially good news, struck him as odd.

He spent the weekend ahead in restless anticipation, wondering what Monday morning held in store. In an attempt to mitigate his anxiety, he kept as busy as possible, doing errands, chores around the house, and working on a research paper for his psychology class. Sunday night brought with it little sleep and a deep sadness. On the precipice of what appeared to be something quite important, Stephen was acutely aware of Lila's absence.

Upon Nat's suggestion he had decided to pursue a teaching career. He had had to rely on his own counsel, and had alone, made a decision that he knew would significantly change his life. Now, another potential decision presented itself. Again, he could not turn to her, Lila, who had always heard the whole of his thoughts and feelings, imbuing them with her own unique perspective. When Monday morning dawned, Stephen opened his sleepy eyes and rubbed them, getting his bearings in a world familiar to him, before heading out the door on a single day's journey that he surmised might permanently change that world.

❦❦

Mr. Sutton stepped out from behind his desk and while holding an unlit cigar in his left hand, extended his right to Stephen. "Hope you had a good trip up, Stephen. Have a seat. Would you like something to drink?"

"No thank you, sir."

"Call me Thomas. Or better yet, Tom will do. George has told me a lot about you. Thinks the world of you."

Stephen looked intently at Tom Sutton, immediately feeling at ease following such a warm reception.

Mr. Sutton leaned back against the front of his desk, looking just as intently at Stephen. "My condolences on your loss," he said, momentarily grimacing. He quickly turned his head to the right and glanced at a picture on the desk.

"Thank you...Tom." From the angle of his chair, situated to Mr. Sutton's left, Stephen could see residing in that picture the smiling face of an attractive middle aged woman.

Thomas Sutton grasped the picture, stared at it and inhaled deeply. "It's been two years," he sighed, his words imbued with sadness. "Time just goes on." He placed the frame back in the exact same spot.

Stephen waited, silently.

"Well, Stephen," he continued, "I guess you're wondering why George and I dragged you all the way up to Boston on a moment's notice. I figure George gave you the bare bones and not the entire story."

It was George Aarons, sitting beside Stephen, who had greeted him when he first entered the office.

Stephen had tried to conceal his shock at the sight of George. Over the years, he had come to know George as a fairly robust man with a contagious smile and light step. Before him had stood a gaunt man wearing an ill fitting suit, his features drawn, his face ashen. After a warm handshake, George had ushered Stephen across the room and then taken a seat to his left.

"Only that it was about a promotion, Tom," interjected George, glancing over at Stephen.

"Why don't you give Stephen the details." Mr. Sutton paused for a second. "As much as you're comfortable with."

George Aarons cleared his throat.

Stephen sat, puzzled over all of the apparent mystery.

"Sorry about all the mystery," began George, as if he had read Stephen's mind. "I'll get right to the point, Stephen. I'm sure you can see, I'm... not well." George took off his spectacles and rubbed his eyes. He then slowly put his glasses back on, continuing to speak. "It's been a battle and there's more, a lot more ahead. That's going to have to be my focus, that and my family. Full time. I've gone as far as I can here." He glanced at Mr. Sutton. "Tom's been very kind, letting me cut back my hours as it is."

Thomas Sutton turned red with embarrassment.

"I wasn't too far from retirement to begin with," continued George, "but now..." George faltered.

No sooner did George pause, than Stephen deduced what was coming. While maintaining his outward composure, inside he swelled with pride.

"I asked George to make a list of recommendations. Best people to run the northeast region."

Mr. Sutton had walked over to George and stood beside his chair. "It was a short list to say the least," he continued. He smiled at Stephen. "You were the only one on it."

George smiled at Stephen as well. "Congratulations. I know I'll be leaving everything in good hands," he said, coughing.

"Stephen, we need you up here as soon as possible," resumed Mr. Sutton, firmly. "I need you tomorrow, but I'll settle for right after New Years. That would give you a couple of weeks to sort things out at home. Of course we'll take care of all expenses, re-location, getting settled in Boston. Anything you need. We can kick all of that around over lunch, the three of us." He paused and walked back to the front of his desk, again looking directly in Stephen's eyes. 'The main point is, the job is yours if you want it." He deliberated for a moment. "I can imagine the year you've had," he said, nodding slowly. "It's a lot to ask, I know. You think about it. Talk to George during the week if you like and let me know by Friday." He turned to George. "Where should we take Stephen for lunch?" he asked, in a lighthearted tone.

Stephen glanced from Thomas Sutton to George Aarons as the two of them discussed lunch. Thomas Sutton struck him as a straight shooter, direct and forceful, though with an empathetic side. Stephen liked the way he treated George. While looking at George, Stephen suddenly recalled a poignant statement George had made several years ago. George had been visiting the bank, sitting in Stephen's office when Mr. Miles called. Stephen remembered clearly what George had said after he hung up the phone. "That's what I miss in my job, Stephen. That kind of human contact. One on one, helping people out. Giving solid advice, a little care besides. A lost art, listening. There are ways of getting to the bottom line without losing sight of people. Not too many left like you, Stephen...or me." Now, as Stephen stared at George, he wondered whether George's regret, if he took the job, could someday be his.

The two men finally turned to Stephen.

"I don't know what to say," Stephen immediately offered, standing and shaking each of their hands. "I'm flattered."

"I didn't expect an answer today," said Mr. Sutton. "I certainly would have welcomed one, but I meant what I said. Take the week."

"Thank you," answered Stephen. "I could use a few days. It certainly would be a bit of a change."

"And that might be a bit of an understatement," said George, putting his arm around Stephen's shoulder. "I'm sorry, Stephen. You would have been my recommendation at any time. I wish it didn't have to be under these circumstances. For me and for you."

"I understand," responded Stephen. "I guess it hasn't been a very good year for either of us. Maybe the one coming up will be better."

"I hope so," grinned George.

"How is Vivian?" asked Stephen.

"She's holding up alright. She's always there, Stephen. She's my anchor. I don't know what I would do without her."

"You're a lucky fella, George."

George looked at Stephen, curiously for an instant, then shook his head in acknowledgment.

"Thanks," he said. "And your...Lila...well you know how Vivian and I felt about her. A real angel..."

"Thank you, George." Stephen took a deep breath at the mention of her name, wondering just what Lila would have thought of all this. Though over the years he'd made a comfortable niche for himself at the bank, he'd often told Lila, without any pressure from her, that if a promotion presented itself, he would give it some thought. That changed with their plans to start a family. He told her then that he would give any offer serious consideration, especially if she wished to stay home for a considerable amount of time to raise their child. And now here he stood, alone, with the most important reason to say yes, gone. The irony was not lost upon him. He wished he could turn back the clock to share this moment with her.

"It's The Four Seasons," said Mr. Sutton, interrupting Stephen's thoughts. "Ever eaten there?" he asked, while placing his unlit cigar in a pristine, crystal ashtray.

"Never," answered Stephen.

"You're in for a treat," added George.

"Splendid!" exclaimed Mr. Sutton, reaching for his overcoat. He waved them towards the door. "Let's go."

❦❦

Suddenly, Stephen heard tapping on the passenger side window. Roused from his reverie and quickly recognizing Nat, he clicked the button to unlock the car door.

With Nat settled in the passenger seat, sneezing and blowing his nose, Stephen pulled away from the terminal.

"Thanks for pickin' me up," Nat said into his handkerchief.

"No problem, Nat. That's some cold. This damp weather is not going to help." Stephen turned on the headlights and windshield wipers as he drove out from under the overhead canopy which extended alongside the arrival's terminal. "It hasn't stopped raining and the temperature already broke a record for the day. Not used to balmy weather in New York this time of year."

"Some fog we're drivin' into. Lucky to land I guess," shrugged Nat. "Wish I felt better. Musta picked somethin' up from the kids."

"How is your family?" asked Stephen, staring intently ahead, concentrating on his driving.

"Grandkids are gettin' bigger and smarter. Growin' up nice. Couldn't be prouder of my boys and my daughters-in-law." Nat sneezed. "How 'bout you, pal? How ya been?"

"I'm alright, Nat," answered Stephen, flatly.

"Don't sound too convincin' to me."

"To me either," agreed Stephen. He leaned forward, hunched over the wheel, watching carefully through the fog for the airport exit.

"Anything I can help ya with?"

"I'm not sure yet. Maybe."

"Just gimme the word, pal."

"Thanks, Nat. So tell me, what happened? I remember that you mentioned something on the phone Friday night."

"Told the boys about Rose."

Stephen momentarily turned his head in Nat's direction. Without saying a word, he quickly turned back, having spied the green exit sign out of the corner of his eye.

"Michael asked me what was new. Figured it was a good opportunity. Always was a straight shooter with the boys. Ida, she brought 'em up well. Always trusted their judgement."

Stephen eased along the curved exit ramp and then slowly merged onto the parkway.

Nat blew his nose again and turned to Stephen.

"Doin' a good job a drivin', pal."

"Thanks, Nat. What happened next?"

"Just told 'em the truth. Said I was lonely and was ready for a little company. Nothin' too serious. Didn't even know if it was gonna happen. It was hard, Stephen. I gotta tell ya. Tried to explain that no one could ever replace their mother. No questions asked. This was just somethin' that felt right...now."

"Not an easy thing to do, Nat. How'd they react?" Stephen's eyes stayed fixed on the road.

"Ya know, pal, they said everything I woulda expected. Those are my boys. Always in their old man's corner. But I saw in their eyes...not sure what...sadness...disappointment...don't know, Stephen. Maybe just surprise, seein' as maybe everybody just got used to the way things a been. I felt bad."

"You always do what you think is right," responded Stephen. "You're always true to yourself and treat everyone fairly. I know your sons love you dearly, Nat...but you deserve a little happi..." Stephen hit the brakes as red tail lights suddenly appeared through the thick fog, barely a few feet ahead of them.

"Whew! Close call!" gasped Nat.

"Lucky no one was behind us," added Stephen, easing back onto the gas pedal.

"Tough night for drivin'. Wouldn't a dragged ya out if I'd a known."

"It's alright, Nat. Don't worry. I'll get us home."

"I know ya will, buddy. Just gotta keep lookin' ahead, eyes on the road. Can't always worry about what's behind. Gotta keep lookin' ahead. Straight ahead til we get outta this fog."

"You're a wise man, Nat," chuckled Stephen.

Nat laughed. He sneezed and then continued laughing.

"Let me in on the joke," said Stephen.

"It's me and you, pal. We're becomin' regular philosophers, the two of us. Just chock full a wisdom."

Stephen joined in the laughter. "So we are," he agreed. "So we are."

❄❄

After what seemed to him an eternity, Stephen pulled up in front of Nat's house.

"Finally," he murmured.

"You're a trooper," responded Nat, opening the car door.

"Let me get your suitcase," offered Stephen.

"Thanks. I'm exhausted."

Stephen retrieved Nat's suitcase from the trunk.

He carried it up the walkway, ascended the front steps, and set it down on the porch.

"There you go, Nat."

"I'm done in, buddy," yawned Nat, "but not so done in that I can't tell somethin's on your mind."

"There is. But you need to get to sleep."

"Sleep'll wait a few more minutes, pal. Just gimme an idea."

"I got offered a promotion yesterday."

Nat's eyes lit up, bright enough to momentarily efface their weariness. "That's great!" he exclaimed.

"In Boston," added Stephen.

"Oh," responded Nat, the weariness quickly returning. "The world's just spinnin' faster and faster. For me and you both."

"It certainly is, Nat," sighed Stephen. "It certainly is. I'll fill you in this week. Alright?"

"Sure, pal."

"Now you need some rest."

Nat reached into his pocket. "You're right. Where'd I put that key?" he asked himself.

"Oh!" exclaimed Stephen, reaching into his own pocket. "I almost forgot. This is for you."

He took out two quarters and handed them to Nat. "They're from Rose. Change from the flower she...I mean you bought."

"Geez!" returned Nat. "Gotta give her a call 'bout that. Get her number, pal?"

"Oops!"

The two philosophers, one young of age and the other young of heart, simply stood there, their mouths momentarily agape before metamorphosing into smiles.

❋❋

"So...now it's airplanes! Ice skating wasn't enough worry. At least you were on the ground. You should fly in the air now!"

"But Ida, I had to go."

"I know," said Ida, her voice a mixture of resignation and sadness. "So much heartache."

Nat sat slumped in his armchair, still wearing his overcoat, his hat resting on his lap. His four day journey had extinguished his last ounce of energy, and he had collapsed onto his chair soon after entering the house, falling into a deep sleep. On the heels of so emotional a trip, with all of its events so fresh in his mind, he dreamed of his beloved Ida.

"I did good. Here I am, back safe and sound. And the boys, their little ladies, all doin' well. And the grandkids! Growin' up in the blink of an eye. It's a wonderful thing." Nat paused for a second. "But you know, Ida," he continued, his voice infused with weariness, "the kids grow up and us, we grow old. Old and then...I guess it's just the nature a things."

"Not another word," admonished Ida, waving her finger at Nat. "I know it's late. You exhausted yourself. It's no wonder. You should sit in a house for four years and then up and go across the country and back on a moment's notice. Never mind old and...ach...you should be proud of yourself! What if your new lady friend should hear you talk like this? What would she think?"

Nat snapped to attention. No longer slumped over, his eyes now opened wide, he gazed in astonishment at Ida's smiling face.

"So," she said, "this should wake you up? This is the Nat I like to see. This is good for my heart."

"You heard what I said at the cemetery?" he asked in a whisper.

"Of course," answered Ida.

"Stephen was right," said Nat. "He knew you heard me."

"Yes, he was. And Stephen's Lila will always hear him."

"You're a wise one, Ida."

"Wise enough to know you should enjoy good company, Nat."

"So, you're not mad?"

"Mad! At you! Never!"

"Thank you, Ida."

"Never mind thank you. I should have to give you advice at your age. Call your lady friend."

Nat scratched his head and yawned. "But it's awful late," he said.

"Ach, not now," said Ida.

"Besides, Stephen forgot to get her number."

"You should only know from a telephone book, Nat."

Nat slapped his forehead with the palm of his hand. "The phone book!" he exclaimed. "Why didn't I...you're a gem, Ida, a real gem."

"So are you," laughed Ida, again waving a finger at him, only this time in jest. "Oh, and Nat," she added, "next time you make my banana bread, maybe a little less cinnamon."

"Will do, Ida," yawned Nat, his eyes slowly closing. "Will do."

When It Rains, It Pours

MORGAN ANDREWS EXITED THE MEN'S room of the Hillwood Community Center, and with great pride, lightly patted the neatly folded handkerchief in his breast pocket. It was a habit of his. A few minutes in front of the men's room mirror insured him that his drive over from Fairfield Heights had not unduly altered the fresh appearance of his impeccable attire. Gazing in the mirror only confirmed to him that his gray worsted wool suit, crisp white shirt, and perfectly knotted tie were as seamlessly arrayed as when he left his apartment. A lifelong bachelor and avid bridge player, he was drawn for the first time to the community center by the breakup of his own weekly bridge game. Married friends who had moved to a warmer climate and the passing of a single friend signified the demise of a longstanding bridge foursome that had brought him much pleasure.

Standing in the hallway, far removed from his quiet foursome, he heard a rising crescendo of voices to his left. He turned and walked to the far end of the hallway, entering the open door of the recreation room.

"Is there anyone who needs a partner?" sounded a voice, barely audible above the loud din.

Morgan walked intently in its direction.

"Thank you, Stella," said Rose.

"You don't have to thank me, Rose. I want you to enjoy the morning and...it's my job."

"Hopefully, Dora will be better by next Friday," responded Rose.

Stella quickly scanned the room and once again shouted out, "Is there anyone who needs a partner?"

Suddenly, to Rose's right a gentleman appeared.

"At your service, madam," said Morgan Andrews.

Both Rose and Stella turned, startled.

"I would be delighted to be your partner." Morgan removed his hat and extended his hand to Rose. "Morgan Andrews is the name."

❄❄

Rose momentarily looked askance at the meticulously dressed stranger with his formal words of introduction. She was struck by the contrast of his staid, measured demeanor with the raucous hubbub surrounding her. Not one to be thrown off stride for very long, she instantly regained her composure.

"Accepted," she responded, reaching for Morgan's hand, grateful for the opportunity to play. "My name is Rose Pierce."

"A pleasure to meet you, Miss Pierce."

Rose smiled. "Rose will be just fine," she said.

"As will Morgan," he smiled back.

"Wonderful!" exclaimed Stella. "Take the two seats at the table with Tess and Lew."

"Thank you, Stella," said Rose.

"Yes, thank you, madam," chimed in Morgan.

"Are you new to the area?" asked Rose, addressing Morgan as they wound their way around the bridge tables on their way to the other side of the room. "You've never been here before."

"No, I live in the Heights," offered Morgan. "I've lost my regular foursome and bridge is my one vice."

"I'm sorry to hear that."

"There are worse vices," laughed Morgan.

"I didn't mean bridge," laughed Rose.

"Ah, you were referring to my foursome. Yes, a dear friend passed away and the other two, old, old friends, needed to relocate to a warmer climate. The afflictions of age, what can one say, Miss Pierce."

"Rose."

"Yes, Rose," responded Morgan, correcting himself.

"Rose!" exclaimed Tess, alarmed at the sight of Rose not only approaching without Dora, but in her stead, with a strange man.

"I'd like you to meet Morgan…"

"Andrews," said Morgan, completing Rose's sentence while extending his hand.

Tess and Lew stood, each shaking Morgan's outstretched hand.

"Your friend Rose was most kind enough to be my partner. I do hope not to disappoint her."

Tess and Lew looked at one another. As they so ably did after fifty two years of marriage, they effortlessly read the wonder written in one another's eyes. Wondering utmost, who was this character of immaculate attire who spoke with such a flourish?

"Pleased to meet you," they said in unison, suspending their curiosity for the moment.

Then turning to Rose, her face registering concern in lieu of wonder, Tess asked, "Is Dora alright?"

"Just a cold," answered Rose. "She'll be back next Friday."

"Have a seat Morgan," said Lew, gesturing to his right. "Glad you could fill in for Dora. Rosie is awfully sharp. I'm sure you'll find it a stimulating morning."

Rose blushed at Lew's compliment.

Morgan pulled Rose's chair out for her. "After you, madam," he said, with a wave of his arm.

"Thank you, Mr. Andrews."

"Please...Morgan. And you are most welcome."

As the compass directions go, they sat opposite one another in the North-South bridge positions. It did not take long for each of them to recognize one another's acuity as players. Despite their North-South position, they were anything but poles apart. In a game requiring a partnership of communication based not on words, but on skilled play, they succeeded beyond what either could have expected after having just met. Their final point total was more than adequate for such a newly formed partnership.

"A most stimulating morning, indeed," said Morgan, addressing Rose as they stood beside the refreshment table after the last match.

"I'm glad you enjoyed your morning here," answered Rose, nibbling on a cookie. Rarely did she forego a sweet or dessert, a self acknowledged weakness of hers.

"Are you as good at dancing as you are at bridge?" asked Morgan, nonchalantly, as he held down the lever of a large coffee urn, filling his styrofoam cup.

Rose stopped chewing as Morgan turned to her with his cup in hand.

"I was reading the flyers on the bulletin board when I came in," he continued. "There's a dance next month. Might I have the pleasure of your company?"

Rose held her almond cookie in mid air, speechless.

"You needn't answer right away," said Morgan. "Perhaps, if you would be so kind, you could give me your number and I could call you. You could tell me then."

"Oh dear," said Rose, swallowing. "Dancing...I haven't danced in...I used to love to dance."

A broad smile crossed her lips, masking a modicum of wariness and uncertainty concerning this stranger whom she had so recently met. "I...I'm not sure...it's been so long," she answered.

"Might I call you then? Just in case our paths do not cross before then."

"Won't you be back next week?"

"I expect that your regular partner, Dora, will return. In which case, I think it would only be a disappointment to play with someone other than you."

Once again, Rose was speechless. The combination of being flattered and admittedly intrigued by a most charming Morgan Andrews dispelled her wariness. She put the remainder of her cookie down on the table and opened her pocketbook, taking from it a pen and tiny notepad. She wrote down her phone number and handed it to Morgan. "Here you are," she said.

"I thank you in advance for your consideration," nodded Morgan, folding the small piece of paper and putting it in his jacket pocket.

Fully regaining her voice, as well as her composure, Rose calmly and confidently responded, "You're welcome, Mr. Andrews.

I'll certainly think about what you asked, but I can't make you any promises."

"I understand." Morgan glanced at his watch.

Rose's gaze was drawn to the glistening gold watchband that enveloped his wrist. It was no less striking than the star sapphire pinky ring on his right hand that commanded her attention when first he dealt the cards. There was much that struck her about Morgan Andrews.

"I must be going," he continued, lightly patting the still very neatly folded handkerchief in his breast pocket. "It has been my pleasure, Miss Pierce." Morgan extended his hand.

"Thank you," responded Rose, grasping his outstretched hand. "I'm glad we were both able to enjoy ourselves this morning."

"Without a doubt," agreed Morgan. He nodded once again. "Have a most pleasant rest of the day," he added.

Rose smiled.

Morgan Andrews turned and walked towards the door.

Rose watched as he wound his way around the bridge tables. She wondered what in the world she was going to tell Dora.

❋❋

As Nat telephoned Stephen on Friday evening from across the country, so too did Dora telephone Rose, only from across the street.

Rose was drying the last of her dinner dishes when the phone rang. She put down the dish towel and reached for the receiver, not surprised by an early evening call.

"Hello," she said.

"Hi, Rosie," sniffled Dora.

"Any improvement?" asked Rose.

"Not much." Dora sneezed.

"Bless you."

"Thank you, Rosie. I can't get rid of this drip. But never mind me. So...tell me about bridge. Who did you play with?"

"Well..." began Rose, "first I should tell you how the day began."

"Oh, my! Something bad happen, Rosie?"

"No, no. Not at all. Remember that sweet man I told you about?"

"Sure. The one you met in the supermarket. We were going to do a little investigating. What's his name?"

Rose laughed. "Nat," she answered.

"Nat," repeated Dora, reaching for a tissue with her free hand.

"I met him...I mean I was supposed to meet him for breakfast this morning but he had to fly to his children in Arizona..."

"Wait a second," interrupted Dora, blowing her nose. "I'm confused, Rosie. Nat...breakfast...what did I miss?"

"I'm sorry," responded Rose, feeling a twinge of guilt at having kept Dora in the dark. "Everything happened so quickly. I thought I would tell you this morning at bridge. When you called and said how awful you felt, I didn't want to keep you on the phone..."

"You could have kept me on the phone all day for that. So, tell me now."

"There isn't much to tell. We had met again in the super-market and he asked me if I'd like to join him for coffee at that little restaurant on Tulip Avenue. To make a long story short, he couldn't make it. He sent a friend to fill in for him."

"Another man now?" Dora's voice rose in amusement.

Rose laughed again. "Forty years younger," she said.

Dora blew her nose again, but not before gasping first. "Did you say forty years younger?"

"A friend of Nat's, Dora," Rose quickly said. "Just to fill in. Very young and so sad. His wife passed away recently."

"I'm so confused...and with this cold...you'll have to sort all this out for me when I'm better. Just tell me about bridge. Did you have a nice time? Who did you play with?"

"Well...that's another story."

"Don't tell me! Another man!"

"Well..."

"Rosie!"

"He just appeared."

"Who?"

"Morgan Andrews."

"Morgan Andrews? From where?"

"The Heights," answered Rose. "His foursome had broken up and he was looking for a partner. He's quite the bridge player and..."

"Don't tell me," said Dora, bracing herself for the next bit of news.

"He asked me if I would like to go to the "Winter Dance" next month."

"Hhhhuh...." Dora drew in all the air that her stuffed passages would permit. "What did you answer?"

"I didn't give him a yes or no."

"But you love to dance, Rosie."

"I know, Dora," sighed Rose. "And he was quite the gentleman. So well spoken. A snappy dresser. He wore a suit. Did you ever see a man wear a suit to the center to play bridge? And I had the feeling that he always dresses like that. Fine jewelry, too."

"So, what was the holdup? Why wouldn't you say yes?" As usual, Dora did not mince words. She had gotten right to the point.

"After meeting Nat...," began Rose.

"The other man?" interrupted Dora. "But you only recently met him, too. Morgan sounds charming."

"Either charming or a charmer," quipped Rose. "No matter which," she continued, "there's something about Nat ...he's awfully sweet...but even more...he's just...just...full of life!"

"Well, there's certainly something to be said for that," agreed Dora, startled by the forcefulness in Rose's voice. "Especially at our age," she added. Dora reached for another tissue and blew her nose again.

"You need to get to bed. We'll talk some more tomorrow."

"First tell me," Dora sniffled, "is it Nat or Morgan?"

"We'll see," answered Rose. "Nothing is for certain in this world, but I've got a good feeling which is the right choice."

"One thing is for certain, Rosie."

"What's that?"

"When it rains, it pours!"

They had a good laugh together before hanging up.

A Lucky Man

NAT TURNED THE KEY IN the lock, gave the knob a quick jiggle, and turned to leave. The storm door slowly closed behind him. As he descended his front steps, he couldn't help but see the bright Christmas lights aglow on the brick tudor directly across the street. As it was only four in the afternoon, dusk had not yet settled. Nat smiled to himself and shook his head. Same old Gus, he thought to himself, likes to turn 'em on before dark and leave 'em goin' til February. "Gotta love that holiday spirit," he said aloud, reaching the end of his walkway. He turned up his coat collar and started walking towards Stephen's house.

Rose Pierce rummaged in her handbag, located her car keys and descended her front steps, holding on to the iron railing. She hesitated a moment before opening the car door and quickly glanced at her watch. Ever practical, she planned for two errands before dinner. "The drugstore and then the bakery," she mused aloud. "I should have enough time before dinner," she laughed. "The essentials, my medication, a seeded rye, and a charlotte russe." As she backed out of the driveway, she pondered her affinity for sweets and wondered whether it wouldn't be wiser to skip the charlotte russe. "Only for a lemon meringue pie," she giggled, putting the car in drive and heading down the street.

❄❄

Stephen zipped his coat, took a deep breath, and looked to his left and then his right. Standing in front of his house, he did not spy a soul on Sycamore Street. He turned left and began his walk. It was three o'clock Thursday afternoon. He knew quite well that in less than twenty-four hours he would need to phone Boston with an answer. Turning the corner, he noticed the young women starting to emerge from their houses. He surmised that they were anticipating the arrival of the school buses bringing their children home from school. As he traversed one corner after another, he passed a growing assemblage of parents milling about on each one.

The yellow school buses started to rumble past. Children began to disembark at the corners.

He watched as he walked, and thought of Lila and of little Emily and wondered how she might be doing with her script. He contemplated being a teacher one day himself, envisioning standing in front of a class and hopefully doing what Lila so ably did. He thought of the life he had had with her and of the one that might have been. He recounted lunch with George Aarons and Tom Sutton, recalling the generous financial proposal made by Mr. Sutton. But it wasn't the discussion of money that struck him most about that afternoon. As it now vividly came to mind, it was Tom Sutton's reaction to his admission. Telling Mr. Sutton of his future plans, of his aspirations to eventually be a teacher and continue in Lila's footsteps, seemed to be the ethical thing to do. He would never deceive anyone, either intentionally or by omission. He knew that he could only accept the job if all of his cards were on the table. At an opportune moment, he had laid them all out. How surprised he was when Mr. Sutton, without so much as a hesitation, looked him in the eye and said, "I appreciate your candor, Stephen. It's a wonderful idea. Admirable. Simply admirable. It doesn't change a thing, though. My offer stands. Life is too unpredictable. The three of us can certainly agree on that. Your plans may change. We'll just cross that bridge if and when we come to it. If you take this job it's yours until the day you tell me it's not." Though initially stunned by this response, so uncharacteristic in the business world he knew, Stephen quickly concluded to himself that it had something to do with the picture of the woman on Mr. Sutton's desk, the one that Tom had sadly held in his hand. She no doubt meant as much to Tom as Lila meant to him. So now he had been offered it all, a promotion without compromising his goal to be a teacher. It would be all his with a simple yes.

Block after block the thoughts kept coming, a plethora of scattered thoughts unable to form a cohesive pattern in so organized a mind. He looked around the neighborhood, at the houses and well manicured lawns. This is my home, he thought to himself. Or is it, without her? A little boy ambled past him, slightly hunched over by the weight of his backpack, his mother by his side. Stephen smiled down at him as the idea of going to night school in Boston crossed his mind. His first course was coming to a close in a week. It had not been a burden to him and even supposing more work related responsibilities in Boston, he did not surmise any problems with continuing on at night.

Slowly but surely he would attain his goal, one course at a time. Boston certainly had plenty of colleges.

And yet, on the other hand…A new city? A new job? A new beginning? Did he really need to make even more adjustments so soon after…? He turned up his collar and put his hands in his pockets. A slight wind was beginning to kick up. Suddenly, a swirl of snowflakes appeared, seemingly out of nowhere. The first snow of the season. They gently descended, encircling him as he continued on. His steps led him past Lila's school and on past the neighborhood park and its empty playground. He traversed the boundary of his immediate world, alone.

Dusk was falling as he turned the corner back onto Sycamore Street and headed up his block, staring at the ground.

"Got the weighta the world on them shoulders a your's, pal."

Stephen looked up, a broad smile crossing his lips in acknowledgement of that familiar voice.

Nat stood directly under the lamppost in front of Stephen's house, the snow falling upon him, flakes gently alighting on his shoulders and the brim of his hat.

"You're a sight for sore eyes," laughed Stephen.

"Thanks, pal."

"What brings you this way?" asked Stephen.

"You, buddy."

Stephen reached Nat and they stood facing one another beside the lamppost. Suddenly, the light above their heads came on.

Through the falling snow, Nat looked at Stephen and then glanced past him towards the front porch of the house.

"Just like the first night. Me and you here. The little lady was standin' up there." He sighed.

Stephen, too, glanced at the porch.

"I miss her, Nat. So much."

"I know you do, pal." Nat put his arm around Stephen's shoulder. "Listen, buddy. I been thinkin'. Remember when you went with me to the cemetery?"

"Sure I do," responded Stephen.

"And you were tellin' me about the big picture and how it's really all these little things addin' up one after another and leadin' ya ta your fate."

Stephen grinned. "I remember. And you asked where it begins."

"Exactly!" exclaimed Nat, overcome with excitement. "And you said, maybe anywhere!"

"I did?" asked Stephen, unable to retrieve that precise moment from a mind of teeming, cascading thoughts.

"You sure did, pal."

Stephen nodded his head. "Well, that makes sense, I guess. You can never truly put your finger right on the beginning. It could be anywhere."

"Exactly! And that's the point!" Nat tipped the brim of his hat slightly up and stared straight into Stephen's eyes. "This is anywhere, pal!"

Stephen's eyes lit up in recognition.

The house adjacent to his suddenly lit up too, its facade ablaze in Christmas lights.

They both stared at it through the swirling snow.

"Holiday is here, pal. A new year comin' up. Maybe it all starts here. A new beginning!" Nat turned his eyes back to Stephen's porch. "No matter what, though, we don't forget…"

"Never," agreed Stephen, tears quickly welling up in his eyes. He wiped them away with his fingertips and just as quickly broke into a broad grin. "You're becoming quite the philosopher, pal."

"Thanks, buddy."

Stephen's grin dissipated. "Listen, Nat, talking about the cemetery, would you do me a favor?"

"Sure, anything for you."

"I'd like to take a ride out…before I…" Stephen faltered.

"I'm with ya, pal. Just say when."

"Thanks, Nat."

"And don't forget about teachin'. Got that pen I gave ya? You'll be needin' it someday."

"I'll give my first A with it," joked Stephen.

"You give 'em all A's, pal. Every kid. All the time. I'd like that."

"You got it."

Nat put his hands in his pockets, drew his arms in close to his sides and shivered slightly. "Gettin' a little cold out," he said.

"Why don't you come in and I'll put up some dinner for us," suggested Stephen.

"Well," began Nat, timidly, "I kinda have dinner plans already. On my way to the restaurant, matter a fact." With a sheepish grin, Nat winked at Stephen.

"Oh," responded Stephen, taken aback, his expression a mixture of wonder and amusement. "In that case…"

"Sorry I gotta run out on ya, pal. You'll take a raincheck? In fact, I'll cook dinner for you before you leave town. Whatd'ya say? Deal?"

Stephen looked at Nat, a true friend whom he knew he would always be able to depend on, no matter when or where. "A deal is a deal," he answered.

"Then I'm off, pal. You let me know how it goes tomorrow." He winked again and began to walk down Sycamore, the lightly falling snow still swirling in the wind, more houses lit with the glow of the Christmas season. Before reaching the corner he turned around, responding to Stephen's voice, hailing him from under the lamppost.

"But I never got you the number!" shouted Stephen. "What happened?"

Nat took his hands out of his pockets and cupped them around his mouth. He mustered all of his breath and shouted out, "The telephone book, pal. The telephone book!"

❦❦

Rose Pierce parked her car directly in front of the restaurant on Tulip Avenue. She was happy to get a spot right in front and was able to wait in the car and keep warm. She was a little bit early, her errands having taken less time than expected. Within minutes of her arrival, Nat appeared, turning the corner onto Tulip and walking in her direction. She got out of the car and met him on the street.

"Hello, Rose. It's me this time." Nat extended his hand.

Rose smiled. "How are you, Nat? Have you caught up to yourself a little?"

They shook hands.

"A little," answered Nat. "It's good ta be home." Nat held the door to the restaurant open. "Here, Rose, let's get out of the cold."

They entered and were shown to a table.

Rose took off her coat.

Nat held out her seat for her.

"Thank you, Nat," she said.

"You're welcome." He sat opposite her. "I guess we shouldn't stay too long. What with the snow and you drivin'."

"That's thoughtful of you, Nat. But don't worry. It wasn't coming down too hard and it's only a few blocks home. We're here, so let's enjoy the evening. In a real storm I'd certainly think twice."

"Sure thing. You never can tell what can happen in a storm."

The waiter approached, empty handed.

"Good evening, Mr. Zeigler. It's been a while. Good evening, madam."

Before either of them could respond, the restaurant's proprietor appeared at their table and stood beside the waiter.

"I just got a call, Mr. Zeigler. A gentleman called, a Mr. Brook. Apparently, your bill is taken care of. He left an open charge and a message for you and I think he said 'the lovely little lady' if I'm not mistaken. Most peculiar. Anyway, he said it's his treat. Enjoy." The proprietor glanced at the waiter, turned, and walked back to the front counter.

Nat stared at Rose.

She sat, bewildered again in the presence of Nat Zeigler.

"That's my pal!" exclaimed Nat, nodding his head and lightly tapping his heart with his fist. "That's my buddy, Stephen."

"You're a lucky man, Nat," said Rose.

"Thank you, Rose."

The waiter cleared his throat. "The usual, Mr. Zeigler?" he inquired. "Half a roast chicken?"

"Rose?" asked Nat.

"I'll have whatever you're having."

"Two half a roast chickens?" inquired the waiter.

Nat looked at Rose. He looked intently at her. He then slowly turned and looked up at the waiter. "I'd like to see a menu," he said, smiling from ear to ear.

THE END